Tales from
My Back Porch

Darrell Case

Darrell Case

Proverbs 11:30
Leaning Tree Christian Publishers
Post Office Box 6124
Terre Haute, IN 47802

Other books by Darrell Case

Live Life to the Fullest

Out of Darkness

Never Ending Spring

Sluagh

River of Fire

Miracle at Coffeeville

Deadly Justice

Hands of The Father

ACKNOWLEDGMENTS

I would be remiss if I did not thank those who worked so diligently for the completion of this book. These are the unsung heroes behind every author. Their names appear nowhere other than in the acknowledgments, yet should be in neon lights.

To my wife, Connie, who sees the value in every story and encourages me to keep going when sales are low and debts are high. To Mary Ellen Robertson, my long-suffering editor who holds my feet to the fire when I'm tempted to let things slide. To Justin and Christina Drake at The Wicked Chicken Homestead for the use of their barn and porch for the cover photos.

To Kim Merrick of God's Country Photography for the magnificent cover design.

To my Lord Jesus Christ, who oversees my writing. The good parts are His, any mistakes are mine. To those of you who prayed for me each morning as I sat down at my computer. And to you, the reader, who makes every pen stroke worthwhile.

Forward

In days gone by, the back porch was reserved for family and close friends. While salesmen and other solicitors were relegated to the front, the rear of the home was less formal. There the women gathered for quilting bees or to exchange recipes. The men of the household would sit and rest on the back step before returning to their chores. A garden hoe or rake might lean against the railing in back, but would never be seen in the front.

In the evening as the sun rode the horizon, the back porch took on an aura of enchantment. Friends and neighbors gathered to chat over tinkling glasses of iced tea. Children chased fireflies and each other, their laugher mingling with the adults' more serious conversations.

As dusk settled and the lamp was lit, the little ones wandered in to sit on the floor or snuggle in their parents' laps. Glasses were refilled and someone would settle back, look up at the stars and say, "I remember when…" Thus began a tale, often embellished with some distant imagining. Regardless, each one taught a lesson of life. Later that night after they were tucked into bed, the children would drift off to sleep remembering the story. Years later they repeated those tales of life to their own child, and so on through the generations.

By the way, I remember when…

For those forgotten by the world,
yet each one is a story.

Darrell Case

Contents

Best Day _____ Pg 1

Skinny Dipping _____ Pg 13

Reverend Dillard's Dilemma _____ Pg 31

Lucille's Library .... Pg 40

A Dog for Sidney .... Pg 50

Mission Bored _____ Pg 68

Crip _____ Pg 85

Millie's Promise .... Pg 98

The Road to Nowhere .... Pg 121

Earl _____ Pg 138

The Best Day

It was raining. A slow, chilly, miserable drizzle soaked the trees, the beach, everything. Droplets ran down the window like tears.

Her face downcast, her eyes moist, Dora stood staring at the gray-green ocean's waves lapping at the shore. She longed to dig her toes into the sand to feel its gritty roughness and the coolness below the hot surface. Her sigh was like a soft sob. The sound tore through Paul like a knife in his heart.

How he loved this woman. He had since the first time he saw her in the student union at Earlham College in eastern Indiana, where the two of them both studied and worked. Dora wore no make-up; her hands were enclosed in latex gloves, her dark blonde hair was tied in a low ponytail under her hairnet. Petite and willowy, she looked even younger than her 18 years. Sensing Paul's eyes on her as she served up meat loaf and mac and cheese to the chattering students, she looked up and smiled. Paul's breath caught in his throat. He managed a foolish grin, hoping she couldn't tell how awkward he felt. It had taken him three weeks to muster the courage to ask her out. He stammered his invitation, the words tumbling out as she gazed quizzically at him. He couldn't believe she said yes. That night after taking her home, he knew she would be his wife.

Through the thick fog, the shore was a hazy, vague outline beyond the hotel parking lot. Watching his bride at the window made Paul want to cry. His heart broke as he slowly flipped the pages of the novel while peering at her over the book's top edge. Giddy with anticipation and excitement, he had sprung his surprise on her as they drove away from the reception. The string of cans the best man had attached to its back bumper clattered behind Paul's 20-year-old Chevy. The limo he had hoped to hire for their trip was impossibly beyond his means. No matter. Dora said she was just as happy as if he were a millionaire. He knew she was telling the truth but still longed to give her the best.

Turning in the passenger seat, Dora stared at him, her mouth agape. "Hilton Head? Really?" Her eyes widened. "How did you know I always wanted to go there? I never thought it would happen."

Paul grinned. "It's my wedding gift to you, Mrs. Davis." He reached over and squeezed her hand. Mrs. Dora Davis. He loved the sound of it. Now she belonged to him. His wife, his love, his world.

"I love you, Paul," Dora said. Leaning over, she kissed his cheek, causing them both to gasp as he swerved precariously toward the ditch. "Sorry, dear," Dora murmured. Fumbling with the radio until it yielded some soft music, she leaned back in her seat, a dreamy smile crossing her face. "I want to run barefoot on the beach and feel the warm sand between my toes and the sun on my back."

Since the day Paul proposed, Dora had dreamed of the

elaborate honeymoon trip she would take with her new husband. Despite Paul's keeping their destination a secret, throughout their brief engagement she spoke of little else. Her enthusiasm was contagious, making him all but forget the sacrifice it had cost him to make her dream come true.

The wind-driven rain started when they crossed the line into South Carolina. "It's just a quick band," he said hopefully, touching her hand. Not speaking, she leaned forward and stared through the windshield. By the time they reached the hotel at Hilton Head, it had slowed to a cold drizzle.

Sometime in the night, Paul felt his bride arise. He watched through half-closed eyes as she pulled back the heavy drapes. In the light from the bathroom, he saw her sad expression.

The rain continued into the morning. As famished as they were dejected, the newlyweds wandered into a small restaurant down the street. Wincing at the prices, they settled on a breakfast of two eggs, sausage and toast. The waitress frowned when they asked for an extra plate. Returning to their room, Paul tried to persuade Dora to put on her bathing suit. "Maybe later," she said, her voice flat. Paul had saved enough to pay for just two days at the Hilton. There was nothing for extras. The small refrigerator in their room was well stocked, but anything they took from it would show up on their bill. Dora sighed as she opened the door and stared longingly at the snacks and soft drinks. Closing it softly, she stepped into the bathroom. Water ran from the faucet into the plastic cup. Paul's heart sank. Was this the way their married life would be, a couple of paupers stumbling around in a rich man's world and facing one disappointment after another? Who was he kidding? Lying on the bed, Paul's veins burned with shame as he realized his over-ambitious pretense. He picked up the John McDonald novel a previous guest had left behind. The pages blurred until he laid it aside.

Paul had wanted to give Dora the best life, starting with their honeymoon. In the weeks leading up to their wedding day, he spent hours flipping through magazines, mooning over vacation spots of the rich and famous. Calculating how much he would need to give her a memorable honeymoon, he almost regretted Dora's accepting his proposal. He couldn't afford even a tenth of what well-off people spent on a room for one night. Begging for overtime at the college, he was rewarded with a few hours' worth. He scrimped and scraped from everywhere. Still not enough.

Aware of the couple's financial straits, their pastor graciously waived his fee for performing the wedding ceremony. Members of the congregation decorated the church. The Ladies Missionary Society catered the meal and even provided a beautiful, three-tiered cake complete with a bride and groom topper.

Dora didn't know but would find out later that Paul had sold his guitar to pay for their stay at this hotel. He bought the Gibson when he was 16, after working all summer putting up hay. That guitar went everywhere with him. He serenaded Dora with it on their first date,. Starry-eyed, she listened intently, awed by his talent. She wanted him to play at their wedding. No. Now he would make music only for her. Dora would be crushed if she knew the guitar was now in the hands of a 12-year-old girl three states away.

Dora stepped out of the bathroom, sniffling and fighting back tears. The bed sagged. Laying the book on the bedside table, Paul turned over and took her in his arms. Her resolve loosening, Dora began to quietly weep. Saying nothing, he held her, caressing her hair until she slept. He prayed silently, asking the Lord for a miracle. An idea came to him. He could ask. The worst they could do was say no. Gently, so as not wake her, he laid Dora's head on the pillow and stood at the bedside watching her sleep. Surely it was not possible for a man to love his wife more than he did Dora.

Paul closed the door softly behind him. Riding down in the elevator, he rehearsed his speech, clasping his hands together to keep them from trembling. His knees wobbled as he crossed the lobby. He almost turned back. No! No matter how humiliating, he must do this for the woman he loved.

"May I speak with the manager, please?"

The front desk clerk looked up. "Certainly, sir. Is everything satisfactory?"

"Uh, yes, yes everything is fine," Paul stammered.

The man stepped away from his station and returned shortly, followed by a distinguished-looking, nattily-dressed middle-aged gentleman who smiled and held out his hand."Good evening, Mr. Davis. I'm Stevenson Hollister, the hotel manager. How may I help you?" The man's suit cost more than Paul's car. He felt shabby and small in his thrift store clothing.

Hollister knew all his guests, the wealthy ones as well as those who had saved for a year to spend a few days at his hotel. He smiled and waited patiently for the young man's reply. Losing his courage, Paul faltered. He opened and closed his mouth, finally managing to mumble, "I... I'm sorry I bothered you." He turned to go back to his room.

"Please, Mr. Davis, why don't we step into my office so we can speak privately?"

Meekly, Paul followed him down a hallway. Hollister opened the door to an office almost as large as the apartment in Indiana where Paul and Dora would live. As soon as the manager closed the door, Paul blurted, "I don't have much money!" He fumbled in the pocket of his jeans, pulled out an embarrassingly small wad of bills and laid it on the gleaming desk.

Sitting down behind the desk, Hollister opened a book with a green cover. "Mr. Davis, I see your room was paid for in advance." He glanced up to see tears forming in the corners of Paul's eyes.

"Yes, the room is paid for, but I wanted to rent one of those little tents on the beach." Paul lowered his head and tried to collect himself.

"Little tents? Oh, you mean a cabana," Hollister corrected with a gentle smile.

"Cabana, yes," Paul felt his face redden. "You see, Dor... my wife, works as a server in the cafeteria at our college and I'm a janitor there. So we didn't have much money for our honeymoon and I sold my guitar just to be able to afford two nights here and..."

Hollister saw the tears about to spill over and understood. In his mind, the kind hotel manager traveled back to when he too was a penniless newlywed. He and his young bride had started on a road trip with just a few dollars between them. They coasted into Garden City, Kansas, on fumes.

Hollister remembered how grateful he'd been to earn enough sweeping the floors of a mom-and-pop store to allow them to continue their journey. He made a decision. Stepping around the desk, he laid his hand on the young man's shoulder. "I see. You want the extras."

"Y... yes." Paul's face flamed. "I can't pay you now. But if we could work something out, I will gladly pay you back, say, in a year or two?"

Hollister leaned over and looked at his book again. "I see you're staying in one of our honeymoon suites?"

"Yes," Paul answered tensely. "Is... is that a problem?"

"Oh, no, on the contrary. It's very beneficial for you and your bride, because all the amenities and meals are included in the price of the room. You're welcome to dine in the restaurant and order anything on the menu. Or if you prefer, you may order from room service." Paul's mouth dropped. He didn't remember seeing anything like that in the brochure. "Everything the hotel offers is included in the price of your room," Hollister assured him. "And you're free to use the cabanas at any time." Paul could only stare in disbelief. Hollister continued, "Perhaps you were unaware of our inclement weather policy for newlyweds. You are welcome to stay two extra days, if you so desire."

"Yes. Yes!" His face lighting up in a huge grin, Paul grabbed Hollister's hand and pumped it. "We can absolutely stay! You don't know what this means to me, sir."

Hollister's smile told Paul what he was thinking: Oh, yes, my young friend, I do. "As for the cabana, please let any member of the staff know when you'd like to reserve one."

"Is it too late to reserve one for later today? Say in an hour?" Paul held his breath.

"I believe that can be arranged."

"Thank you, Mr. Hollister. Thank you so much!" Paul turned to leave.

"There's just one thing," Hollister said.

The young man's face fell. There it was. The manager had been making fun of him. None of what he told him was true. In school, the bullies had pulled pranks on him, but of all the suffering he had endured, this was the cruelest. Stiffly, he turned to face the man, bracing for the ridicule he would heap on him. Whatever mockery he would endure for Dora's sake, Paul vowed never to burden her with it. Smiling, Hollister held out the few dollars Paul had placed on his desk. Weak with relief, Paul took the bills and stuffed them into his pocket. "I'll see that cabana number four is available for you and Mrs. Davis within the hour," Hollister said. "Please enjoy your stay, and if there's anything else you need, don't hesitate to call." He handed Paul an embossed business card.

Paul stumbled through the lobby, followed by the stares of bemused fellow guests. By the time he reached the elevator he had recovered and, too excited to wait for the pokey conveyance, fairly flew up the stairs.

Stevenson Hollister stepped to the front desk. "Mr. Norris, about the young man who just left my office."

"Yes sir?"
"Please mark his bill paid in full and put his other charges

on my account."

"Yes sir."

The two men exchanged knowing smiles. Unbeknownst to corporate, Hollister's largesse was extended to dreamy-eyed newlyweds several times a year.

Winded from climbing the stairs, Paul hurtled through the door of their suite, startling his bride. Awakened from her sorrowful sleep, Dora sat bolt upright. Breathless, Paul panted, "Darling, I have great news."

"What is it? Tell me quick," Dora said, her eyes wide.

"Everything is paid for. The cabana, our meals, even the stuff in the refrigerator."

"What? How is that possible?"

"I talked to the hotel manager. Everything's included in the price of the room. And because of the rain, we can stay 'til Friday!"

Dora leaned her head against Paul's chest and began to cry. But her tears of sorrow now became tears of joy. She lifted her head and met the love in Paul's eyes with a brilliant smile. He thought it was the most beautiful sight he'd ever seen. Maybe this was their turning point. His anxiety over one disaster after another following them through life had vanished.

"Let's celebrate!" Dora exclaimed. Jumping up from the bed, she went to the refrigerator and took out two small ice cream cakes and two cans of soda. Seated at the table by the window, they were barely aware of the rain. Paul leaned over to kiss the ice cream mustache off Dora's upper lip. She giggled. Their eyes locked and his heart nearly burst. He didn't think he could love her more than he did at this moment. The years ahead would prove him wrong. Forty-five minutes later, the two ran barefoot down the beach in the light shower.

Watching them from the window of his office, Hollister smiled. "So much in love," he said softly. Stepping to his desk, he picked up the phone and dialed room service. "John, a couple will be dining shortly in cabana number four. Please make sure they understand they may order whatever they wish. Yes, charge it to their room."

As Paul and Dora reached the cabana, the rain stopped. Seconds later the sun emerged from behind the clouds. A radiant rainbow spread across the sky, its ends seemingly anchored in the blue-green ocean. The waves lapping at the beach sounded to them as sweet as any love song.

"Look dear, God is smiling down on us," Dora said, her face lit up with a gorgeous smile.

"He certainly is, sweetheart. He certainly is." Taking his bride in his arms, Paul kissed her.

Fifty-five years later

The frail elderly woman sat next to the elegant casket, caressing its golden oak finish. She smiled through her tears at the young couple standing before her. Newly married and so much in love, they reminded Dora of her husband and herself. She sent a silent prayer to heaven that these two would never lose their passion for each other. They had stopped by the funeral home on their way to a couples' retreat. He was a rising star in the corporate world, she a budding social butterfly. They came to pay their respects to the couple they regarded as the picture of a perfect marriage. Her face radiant, the wife asked Dora, "What is your happiest memory?"

With a whimsical smile, Dora thought of the financial struggles. The electronics business she and Paul spent a year planning and actualizing from the living room of their modest rental home. The mistakes and missteps on the way to the company's going national, then global a few years later. Their trips abroad, staying at the most beautiful hotels. Dancing under the stars in Paris with her beloved husband. The births of their three children. The magnificent home Paul built for her at the edge of their private lake. All the laughter and good times.

"Oh, my dear, in our fifty-five years together there are so many," Dora said, her face beaming. "But I think the most memorable, the best time, was when we were on our honeymoon at Hilton Head." Quietly recounting how a kind hotel manager took pity on a penniless couple, tears misted Dora's eyes as she said simply, "That was truly the best."

The young couple went away astonished. How could this wealthy widow believe the best time of her life was when she and her husband were dirt poor? How could that be better than the limos, the big house and all the other luxuries only the well-heeled could afford? Watching them leave, Dora prayed they would learn the secret to true happiness as she and Paul had.

The next morning Dora arose to a silent, lonely house. The children had returned to their homes to live their lives until they too would face a day such as this. Dora had given the staff the day off. She wanted to be alone with the memory of the one her heart longed for, the one who had devoted his life to her.

Hobbling on her cane, Dora made her way to the small room at the back of the house where the view of the lake was unobstructed. The secluded nook held so many happy memories. Seated on the reupholstered couch they brought from their first apartment, she thumbed through the family photo album until she found the picture of a smiling young couple on the beach. Tracing her husband's face with a trembling finger, Dora whispered, "Yes, my dear, that was the best day."

Skinny Dipping

He waited, his eyes fixed on the bobber. An expert angler, he knew just the right time to set the hook. He had fished all over the world, hauling in some of the most exotic catches. Today he was in his favorite spot, a rushing stream shooting off the Amazon. The place was so fertile he was even willing to brave the threat posed by a nearby colony of cannibals.

What was that? Something moved to his left. Was that a pair of eyes peering through the foliage? He loosened the strap on his holster. Despite the danger, he kept his focus on the fish. He slipped out the Luger and held it in his left hand, ready for action if they rushed him. His aim was just as deadly with his left hand as his right.

Just a few seconds more and he would land his fish. Then he would fight his way through the swirling current to the seaplane he'd left anchored a hundred yards beyond. The red and white bobber disappeared below the surface. He tensed, his muscles tightening. He yanked the pole with just enough tension to set the hook. Too much and he would lose the fish. He jerked the line, setting the hook. He had it.

The arapaima was a monster, the biggest he'd ever seen. Its glistening scales flashed in the bright midday sun; its body arched in a curve. It had to weigh more than 250 pounds. Of course, he would release the fish after bringing it to shore and documenting its weight and length.

Just as he planted one foot on the sandy bank, the cannibals attacked. They came at him from all directions. Gripping the pole in his right hand, he aimed and fired at the one closest, dropping him in his tracks. Fighting the fish with one hand and the cannibals with the other, he emptied the Luger. Miraculously, he killed them all, reeled in the biggest fish he'd ever caught, and exited his adventure by tumbling out of his chair.

"Thank you, Jesse." Miss Fern Ransford could somehow make her voice sharp and gentle at the same time. "I was just about to ask you to join us back on earth, but you saved me the trouble."

Jesse McCann looked nonplussed and somewhat disoriented as the schoolroom erupted with laughter. During the years Jesse had been her student, Miss Fern had come to know him as a bright, imaginative and adventurous boy. With Jesse, she walked a fine line of mentorship in her attempts to encourage his creativity while holding his attention to the subject at hand. She tried not to smile. "Please come up to the board and calculate the sum."

It was the last day of school. The weather was more like mid-summer than late April. Sunlight blazed through the leaves of the huge elms outside the open classroom windows, its beams bouncing off the tile floor and making the children restless. Birds perched on the branches chattered and trilled with happy abandon, adding their music to the day. A gentle breeze ruffled the papers on the desks.

"Yes, ma'am," Jesse said, getting clumsily to his feet. Walking to the front of the classroom amid snickers, he studied the question, hesitated for a moment, picked up the chalk and wrote the correct answer. Not that it mattered, his classmates' minds were on everything but schoolwork. Most of the faculty and many parents had long believed that building the school within sight of the river had been a mistake.

"Thank you, Jesse." Surveying her students, Miss Fern made a decision. "Please take out your readers. I have an assignment for you." Groans echoed through the room. Faces anticipating freedom fell. Miss Fern only gave writing assignments when she expected them to be turned in the next day.

The children placed their McGuffey readers on their desks and waited. Miss Fern paused. This was her last act as an elementary school teacher. In the fall, she would begin teaching English at the new high school in Sullivan. "Your writing assignment is…" A bright smile lit up her face. "Write a one-page essay on… what I did this summer! Class dismissed!" A chorus of cheers ricocheted off the walls. Making a beeline for the door, the children lined up to say goodbye to their teacher. Standing beside the open door, a misty-eyed Fern Ransford hugged each one until they wriggled free to make their escape. The boys fidgeted with embarrassment, yet from the smallest to the oldest every one embraced her. Some of girls were bawling.

Within minutes the schoolhouse was empty. Fern circled the small room, taking down the children's crudely drawn pictures from the walls. Laying them neatly on her desk, she looked around. How many boys and girls had traveled through her classroom on their way to taking their place in society? In the fall someone new would be guiding them. She could only hope it would be with the same degree of interest and care. Fern laid her head on her desk and let flow the tears she'd been holding back all morning. Then she dried her eyes and began the last day's ritual of marking report cards, cleaning the desks and washing the blackboard.

Letty McCann had just hung the last pair of trousers on the line when Jesse streaked past her. Before she could say a word, he vanished into the house, reappearing seconds later with his fishing rod and tackle box.

"What are you up to, Jesse?"

The boy skidded to a halt. Clearly out of breath, he panted, "Sorry, Ma, I didn't see you there. Miss Fern let us out early."

Fern Ransford had been Miss Fern for 20 years, even though she'd been married to Jim for the last 15. Childless herself, Fern treated each child in her class like her own. Her students loved her, as did their parents. Her standing in the community was one of deep regard.

Letty didn't doubt for a second that Jesse was telling the truth. For the most part, he was a good boy, always considerate and honest, if a bit rambunctious. Letty smiled at him. "Your father's in the south field fixing the hole in the fence where the heifer got out. Stop and tell him where you're going."

"Okay," Jesse said, hoping his father wouldn't ask him to help.

"Let me get you a couple of pieces of chicken and a jar of water before you go." Letty started toward the house.

"Oh, Ma, I'll be all right." Jesse was anxious to get going. His best friend, Ralf, would be waiting. Ralf Thomas was the poorest boy in the neighborhood. Jesse had befriended him when no one else would.

"I don't want you drinkin' that river water. You hear me?"

"Yes ma'am." Jesse scuffed at the dirt with his bare feet. How long would this take? And how did his mother expect him to handle all that stuff?

She came back toting a neatly packed burlap sack. "Now you be careful. Don't fall in and don't get your clothes dirty." She knew he would. Her voice became more stern. "And no skinny dippin'! Once was enough for Miss Fern to see more of you boys than she wanted to."

Jesse's face turned crimson. That day the boys thought their teacher had gone home. They were wrong. "Go on, get out of here and have fun." His face still flaming, Jesse took off running. "And bring me back some fish!" Letty called behind him. He waved the pole to let her know he'd heard. Rounding the barn on the run, he detoured to the field where his father was working, not because he wanted to but because he was an obedient son.

Charles looked up from hammering in a staple. Just a bit more and he'd be done. Seeing the fishing pole and burlap sack flapping against Jesse's sides, he said with a teasing grin, "Oh, good, you came to help."

"Miss Fern let us out early." Jesse smiled up at his father's weathered face.

Charles drove in another staple. "So you goin' fishing or helping me fix this fence?"

"The fence will be here tomorrow," Jesse said, knowing his father was ribbing him.

"True, but the cows won't unless I fix it. Bring us back some fish, hear? I'm hankering for a mess of fried catfish tonight. Ralf goin' with you?"

"Yes sir." Jesse slung the sack over his shoulder and headed off.

"You boys have a good time and mind you, be careful around that river. I don't want to have to do all the summer work by myself."

"We will!"

Charles smiled as he watched his boy sprint down the dirt lane. Oh, to be young again and have no worries. He thought of his own childhood. When he was Jesse's age he had spent hours at the very place on the river where the boys would fish today. Tightening the barbed wire across the opening, he hammered the last staple home. "That should hold you, ol' heifer," he told the cow grazing a few yards away.

Jesse ran with a heart full of joy. Summer stretched before him like an endless highway. September seemed light years away. The sun was bright, the sky was blue and he was free. Approaching the river, he saw Ralf waiting on the bank. The boy's clothes were clean but threadbare and ill-fitting. Ralf's father had no money for clothes. Every penny he got his hands on, he spent on liquor.

Occasionally Zach Thomas would swear off drinking and try to clean up his life. He would go for days without a beer. The days he was sober he worked like a dervish, alcohol purging from his pores in a thick, heavy sweat. The odor was unbearably noxious. But eventually he gave in to the craving, drinking himself into a stupor. When that happened, Ralf made himself scarce. The boy's mother died of typhoid fever four years ago, when Ralf was six. Zach never grieved or reconciled with her death. He used alcohol to try to forget. It never worked. Truth was, he moved out of their bedroom and left it as it was the day she died. Although not outwardly unfriendly, he avoided human contact as much as possible. As for the boy, he seemed mostly to just be in the way.

Because of Zach's neglect, Ralf became the neighborhood waif. In the summer, he slept in barns of neighboring farms. Come morning each farmer knew to check the piles of hay before plunging in his fork. Cut from the same cloth as his father, Ralf stayed aloof from others. Jesse was the only one who persisted until they finally became best friends. Ralf came to school if he felt like it, but most days he didn't bother. To everyone's surprise, he showed up today, but only so as to not forfeit their fishing date.

The two boys sat in silence, their eyes fixed on the bobbing corks. Miss Fern watched from the schoolroom window, her heart aching for Ralf. Concerned for the boy's welfare, Fern had approached Zach earlier in the year.

"I ain't never had no education and I turned out a'right," the bleary-eyed man had argued.

"Don't you want more for your son, Mr. Thomas?"

"I ain't gonna make him go to school lessen he wants to," Zach snipped, waving his half-empty beer bottle at her. "An' you, Missy, you can just mind yer own beeswax."

At Miss Fern's behest, the sheriff visited Zach a couple of times to persuade him to make Ralf go to school. Ralf came a few times, then dropped from sight. Fern asked the sheriff to intervene again. His response was less than accommodating. "Look, Miss Fern, it doesn't work with that kid and I got better things to do than traipse all over the countryside looking for some little delinquent you can't keep in your school."

As Fern stood watching the two friends squatting on the

riverbank, she saw Jesse put his arm around the smaller boy. They seemed to be deep in conversation.

'Why don't you come this Sunday?" Jesse coaxed. "Church ain't that bad." Suddenly his bobber was yanked below the surface. He pulled his arm from around Ralf's shoulder and grabbed his pole. The catfish leapt from the water. Ralf jumped to his feet. Already standing, Jesse fought the fish. "Wow! Look at the size of it, Ralf! Must be at least five or six pounds!"

The smaller boy smacked his lips. "Sure gonna make some good eatin'."

Their talk forgotten, the two boys worked to bring the fish to shore. Wading into the water, Ralf grabbed the line. The catfish snapped to life, wiggling and twisting and fighting the hook. Hauling it onto the bank, both boys pounced on it. Together they wrestled it into the burlap bag and dragged it a safe distance from the water.

Jesse looked down at his wet, muddy pants. "Boy, my Ma's gonna be mad. She let me stay in my school clothes and I was s'posed to keep 'em clean."

With a sly grin, Ralf poked his friend with his elbow. "Hey, I know! Sun's hot. Let's go skinny dipping'. We can wash your pants and shirt, then lay 'em on the bushes to dry."

"No way!" Jesse shouted. "Remember last time? Miss Fern saw us? I go skinny dippin' and somebody sees me, I'm gonna be in a heap'a trouble."

"Nah. She been gone a while. I saw her leave," Ralf said persuasively.

"You sure?" Jesse squinted at Ralf. The kid was known to stretch the truth.

"Sure I'm sure. Don't believe me? Go look for yourself."

"I will." Turning, Jesse ran to the schoolhouse. Standing on tiptoe, he peered through the classroom window.

Fern Ransford always enjoyed the quiet time after the students left. Today, though, she was melancholy. For the first time, tidying the schoolroom seemed drudging. Still, she took her time with it, reluctant for the day to end.

Scanning the room through the window, Jesse couldn't see the teacher. She was on her hands and knees scrubbing a stubborn stain between two rows of desks. Letting out a whoop, he raced back to the river. Fern straightened up just in time to see him scooting back to his comrade. She watched in disbelief as the boys stripped off their clothes and bent down to swish them in the river. After spreading the clothes on some bushes, they jumped into the water.

It wasn't their nudity that bothered Fern, it was their disobedience. They had been warned not to go swimming naked. That portion of the river was too public. Fern put away her cleaning supplies and marched down to the riverbank. The boys were so involved in splashing each other they didn't notice her.

"Boys!" Fern shouted in her sternest tone.

Shocked, Jesse scrunched down until only his head was above the water. Under water from his chest down. Ralf grinned sheepishly. "Guess I was wrong," he muttered. "Hi, Miss Fern!"

"I'm going to turn my back and I want you boys to get dressed." Fern turned and stood with her arms crossed.

"But our clothes ain't dry," Ralf shouted above the babbling water.

"That's not my problem. Just get out of there and get your shirts and pants on. NOW!"

Stepping from the water, Jesse grabbed his wet clothes and struggled into them while frowning at his friend. Ralf grinned back at him. So they got caught. So what?

Giving the boys about a minute to dress, Miss Fern turned to face them. Jesse had never seen her angry before. It scared him.

"Ralf, go home and tell your father I will come by to speak with him."

"He ain't home."

"He ISN'T home."

"That's what I said, he ain't home."

Fern sighed. "Well, when he gets home please tell him to come see me."

"Okay," Ralf said with a cocky grin. His old man wouldn't care. The boy considered the incident a non-starter.

Jesse, however, looked as if he were about to bawl. Fern laid her hand on his shoulder. "Come along, Jesse."

Tears glistened in the boy's eyes. "Do you hafta…? I'll tell them, Miss Fern."

Fern pursed her lips to keep from smiling. She was sure he would, but the question was when. "Come on. It won't be that bad."

"Can I get my fish?"

"Go ahead."

Sweeping the back porch, Letty noticed them coming across the pasture and instantly knew something was wrong. Jesse's head was hung low and she could tell he'd been crying. The thought flitted through Letty's mind: Something's happened to Ralf. Watching Jesse trudging along in his wet clothes, she was sure poor Ralf had drowned. The fear of it gripped her.

Fern raised a hand in greeting. Laying down the broom, Letty ran and met them by the chicken coop. "Jesse has something to tell you," Fern told her, gently pushing the boy forward. He looked pleadingly from one to the other. "Go on," Fern prompted.

"Me and Ralf–"

"Ralf and I," Fern corrected.

"Ralf and I went skinny dippin'," Jesse said, his face flaming. Big tears formed in the corners of his eyes and rolled down his cheeks.

Letty gasped, mostly from relief. It could have been worse, a lot worse. After speaking to Letty for a few minutes to relate what she had seen, Fern left for home. After instructing Jesse to change his clothes, hang the wet ones on the line and go to his room, Letty went back to her sweeping.

An hour later when his father opened the bedroom door, Jesse popped to his feet like a soldier at attention. Charles motioned to the boy to sit beside him on the bed. "Do you know why you're in trouble?"

"For skinny dippin'?" Jesse mumbled.

"No," Charles said, laying his hand on Jesse's shoulder. "Every boy I know has gone skinny dipping at one time or another. You disobeyed. You were told not to go swimming naked. Isn't that right?"

"Yes sir," Jesse said, hanging his head meekly. "But Ralf said he saw Miss Fern leave."

"That's not the point, son. What if one of the girls from the school had walked past and seen you? Make no mistake about it. You're being punished for disobeying."

"What are you going to do?" Jesse asked through his sniffles.

Charles stood and walked to the door. After thinking for a moment, he turned to face his son. "I'm going to let you pick your own punishment." He left the room without closing the door.

Ralf. If it hadn't been for him I wouldn't be in trouble, Jesse thought. But he knew that wasn't true. He had made the decision to disobey. He could have told Ralf no. And why did he believe Ralf's claim that Miss Fern was gone? The kid had lied to him before. There was that time last summer when Ralf swore he saw a giant snake under the outhouse floorboards. Jesse pulled up nearly every one looking for the reptile. There was no snake, and his attempt to fix the floor ended with his father having tear out the whole mess and lay a new one. Worse, Jesse was the only who got into trouble. When confronted, Ralf said it just a joke. A good one, too, that he didn't let Jesse live down for the rest of the summer.

Now Jesse sat on the edge of his bed and tried to think of some punishment that only his parents would think severe. All he could come up with was a spanking. At least it would be over with quickly. He heard his mother calling him for supper. At the table, both parents reached for his hands as they bowed their heads. After thanking the Lord for His provision and safekeeping, Jesse's father asked, "Have you thought of a proper form of punishment?

"A spanking?" Jesse answered weakly.

"No," Charles said. "You would remember a spanking only for a short time. I'm looking for something you won't forget, ever." Jesse kept quiet. He had learned in situations such as this it was best not to speak. Finally, Charles said, "The school house could use a coat of paint."

Jesse's face fell. He stared at his father in disbelief. "What? Paint the whole school? That'll take me 'til next year." Now he knew how a prisoner condemned to death felt. Yesterday the summer stretched before him like an unblemished sheet. Now its only promise was sweat and misery. "Can't I just get a spanking? It'll take me the whole summer to paint the school."

"No, Jesse. You're too old for spanking. Besides, you need to learn that there are lasting consequences when we do wrong."

"But, Dad, paint that whole school by myself?"

"No. I'm going to speak to Ralf's father and he'll be helping. And you two won't be painting. The school board has hired a man to do that. He'll start next month. You and Ralf will be scraping and preparing it."

"It won't be as bad as it sounds," Letty said with a sympathetic smile. "And I would imagine you two will think twice before you go skinny dipping in public again."

"That's for sure," Jesse said, relieved and not. It was going to be one long, boring month.

Surprisingly, Ralf's father was sober when Fern met him

outside the hardware store. She explained the situation. "Yup, might just be good for him," Zach agreed. He's been gettin' a little too big for his britches lately. I'll have him at the school at eight tomorrow mornin'."

Jesse picked at his breakfast. Every year he looked forward to the first full day of summer vacation. He and Ralf had begun a month ago planning what they would do on this day. It would be spent fishing and swimming and, if they could talk their parents into it, camping overnight in the woods.

Three weeks before the school year ended, the two boys started scouting places to set up camp. They found the perfect spot a mile upriver. They visited the new campsite three or four times a week. With the days warm but the nights still cool, they gathered firewood and debated over the best place to pitch the tent.

Now their plans were on hold for doing something stupid. Jesse started down the road to the schoolhouse, dragging his feet. As he came within sight of the clearing, he saw Ralf staring dumbly at the building. He held a wire brush in one hand, a putty knife in the other. Hearing Jesse, he turned, his face scrunched into a scowl. "Ain't this somethin'. All this fuss over a little skinny dippin'."

"It wasn't the skinny dipping," Jesse said, laying his tools beside the steps.

"What then?"

"Disobeying."

"Disobeying?" Ralf echoed derisively. "Heck, I do that all the time."

"Yeah, and this is where it got us." Jesse looked at his

friend with exasperation. "Well, iff'n we don't wanna spend the whole summer messin' with this, we better get going."

All morning they worked scraping and brushing. Flakes of dried paint fell into their hair and the grass at their feet. They worked side-by-side, not speaking, then on separate sides of the building, then together again. Jesse kept switching his tool back and forth from one aching hand to the other. They took several breaks that morning. Jesse balled his fist and shook it at Ralf when he suggested they go skinny dipping. Stepping back in mock fear, Ralf grinned clownishly at his friend. "Ah, c'mon. I was just funnin'."

Slipping around the schoolhouse to the pump, Jesse filled a bucket with cold well water. Sneaking up behind Ralf, he dumped it over the boy's head. Ralf jumped and squealed as if he'd been shot. Jesse doubled over with laughter. In retaliation, Ralf picked up the bucket and chased Jesse, splashing what water was left onto his pant legs. After the water fight, the boys returned to scraping the peeling paint off the building. Jesse was near tears when he realized how little progress they had made. "We'll be here til Christmas," he muttered.

As the sun climbed the sky, the boys' commitment dissolved along with their energy. At noon, they laid in the shade of the tree by the tool shed, commiserating over their fate and their red, blistered and sore hands.

"I ain't never goin' skinny dippin' again," Ralf said unconvincingly.

"Me neither," Jesse said, meaning it.

"Well, glad to see you boys did some good work this morning." Jesse opened his eyes to see his father smiling down at him. Behind him, Ralf's father and Jim Ransford stood inspecting the schoolhouse. Jesse sat up to see Fern and Letty spreading a blanket on the ground under one of the large elms.

"We figured you boys would be hungry after working all morning," Jim said, smiling.

"And we thought you would have learned your lesson," Charles added.

"That's for sure," Jesse said, propping himself up on his elbows. Ralf nodded sleepily.

"You guys must be starved," Jim said. "Come on, let's eat."

After a short prayer, they dove in. Halfway through the meal, Zach cleared his throat and looked Ralf in the eye. "Son, I been doin' you wrong. I let alcohol have its way with me. It had me in a trap."

"It's all right, Dad."

Zach shook his head. "Nope, it ain't. I let you and the whole neighborhood down." He took a deep breath. "But with your help and the Lord's, I'm gonna change." Father and son smiled at each other.

"Listen," Charles said, "we better hurry if we're going to finish this by nightfall." The boys stared at him. The grownups laughed. "You boys have learned your lesson."

The boys grinned. "Yes sir!" they said in unison.

Contrary to the afternoon bringing more slavish misery as the boys had expected, it turned out to be a time of laughter and fellowship. With everyone pitching in, the building was scraped and ready for painting by 4:30.

"So, I s'pose you boys are wore out?" Zach said as he gathered the tools into a burlap sack.

"Yes, sir, we sure are," Jesse said, plopping down on the ground.

"Too tired for camping?" Charles asked.

"Nope, ain't too tired for that!" Ralf said, jumping to his feet. Jesse got up a little more slowly. He never wanted to miss a chance to go camping. Truth be told, though, his hands, back and legs ached horribly. Sleeping on the hard ground wouldn't help them.

"Your daddies thought you might say that, so they set up camp for you this morning." Letty said with a wink. "In that place you found down by the willows." Puzzled, the boys stared at her. They were sure they had kept the new campsite a secret.

The grownups laughed. "You gotta learn not to whisper so loud," Zach told them.

"And I have something for you," Miss Fern said. Reaching under a folded blanket, she pulled out a sign and held it up to the boys. In bold black letters on a bright red background, it read:

Warning
Boys Skinny Dipping

"Now whenever you boys decide to swim nude, you post this sign," Charles said.

"And never in view of the schoolhouse," Miss Fern said, smiling. "I've seen more of you boys than your teacher ever should."

The adults laughed. In spite of their embarrassment, Ralf

and Jesse grinned.

That night as they lay under the stars, the boys contemplated their future. Drifting off to sleep, they promised to always be best friends.

Years later, Jesse hunted through the tool shed until he found it. The board was weathered but, though faded with age, the wording was still legible. Jesse had a fleeting thought of repainting it, but decided against it. He wanted to keep this memory of his favorite teacher just as he received it. Jesse and Ralf made use of that sign for many a summer until they were in their late teens. Until today, though, he had no reason to think of it.

Hearing the Model T puttering up the lane, Jesse tucked the sign under his arm and went to meet their new church pastor. Jesse's son, Alex, came running from behind the barn where he'd been feeding the cows. Pulling to a stop, Reverend Ralf Thomas lifted his hand in greeting. In the back seat, Ralf's 10-year-old son, Peter, waved excitedly. Fairly bouncing with excitement, Alex returned his friend's greeting. Laying his hand on Alex's shoulder, Jesse handed him the sign. "Here, son, you'll need this." Taking the sign Miss Fern had given his father years before, Alex read it and grinned.

Reverend Dillard's Dilemma

His paintbrush dripping, Jeff Dillard tottered to the bench under the shade of the large pin oak at the back of the church. Collapsing onto its seat, he surveyed the results of his last four hours of labor. In the afternoon sun, the cracked weatherboard gleamed with the new coat of white paint, but only halfway up. That was as far as Jeff could reach. From there to its steeple, the church was dull gray. Jeff had painted around the building four times. Having seen not a drop of paint in years, the parched wood gulped it in greedily with each brush stroke.

At five-foot-seven, Jeff could only reach so far. He'd used the stepladder, but at 70 he had no intention of climbing an extension ladder. Wearily, he got to his feet and walked around the building. There was no ignoring the punishment time had inflicted upon it. Three coats of paint couldn't camouflage the front door's crookedness; the windows were out of kilter, and the steeple leaned at least six inches off center.

When he became pastor of Wayside Baptist near Bramble, Indiana, Jeff viewed it as a way to remain useful in his retirement. The makeup of the small congregation, mostly farmers and farmhands, was a drastic departure from that of the larger churches he had pastored over the past 35 years. At those churches, Jeff never had to get involved with maintenance. The staff took care of the mowing, painting and repairs.

"We been meaning to get around to fixin' her up," was the response from the head deacon when Jeff mentioned the condition of the building. Jeff scheduled a workday. Two women showed up. He bought boards with his own money to replace the rotted ones and found himself resenting it. He wasn't merely tired, he was spent, body and spirit. He threw the paintbrush down in frustration and disgust. "They don't care what your house looks like, Lord. And apparently neither do you." He didn't bother to replace the lid on the paint can. "Let it dry up for all I care," he muttered.

Leaving the church yard, the dejected pastor walked the half mile to the small Craftsman style cottage he and his wife rented six months ago. Margaret had been thrilled with the home's character and charm. The grounds provided plenty of space and even a potting shed for her to pursue her love of horticulture. It had all seemed so full of promise. Her husband would take this church and build it up as he had the others. He hadn't counted on being met with such lackadaisical attitudes by its members.

Jeff washed as much paint off his hands as he could in the cold water from the outside spigot. Walking to the back of the house, he saw Margaret on her knees pulling weeds in the garden. She straightened up, pressing her hands into the small of her back. He stood for a while, watching her. Like the flowers Margaret so lovingly tended, she had blossomed. Gone was the city pallor, her skin now tanned from spending hours in the garden. Her face eased of tension lines, she looked 10 years younger. Hearing Jeff approaching, she turned and smiled. "Want to help weed the beans?"

"No. I want to quit," he answered flatly.

Margaret's face fell but she kept her head down, poking half-heartedly at the soft soil with the garden claw. "Oh, Jeff, you don't mean that. You have to give them more time. They're country folks, more laid back than what we were used to in the city."

In truth, Margaret liked the slow pace of country life–the quiet road with its sparse traffic, the sounds of birds and buzzing insects uninterrupted by blaring horns and screeching tires. She loved the luxury of sleeping late and waking to the sounds and scents of nature outside their open window. She had planted a bevy of flowers the first week of May, followed a few weeks later by a vegetable garden. Catching the spirit of her enthusiasm, Jeff had made use of the tiny workshop at the back of the property to build birdhouses and feeders, hanging them on trees near the house. Now he wanted to leave their tranquil little place?

"If they get any more laid back they'll be lying on their backs," he said sarcastically. "The church is falling down around their ears and they don't see the need for repairs."

Close to tears, Margaret shaded her eyes with her hand and looked up at him. "Please tell me you don't really want to leave here."

Jeff softened. Pulling her gently to her feet and taking her in his arms, he said, "No, dear, of course not. I'm just worn out." He kissed her, thinking of the day 45 years ago when he asked Margaret to marry him. In his eyes, she hadn't changed much. Or maybe the change was so gradual he never noticed. To Jeff, Margaret's gray hair and wrinkles were her badge of honor.

Sure, he loved her when they first married. Those first years were priceless. He couldn't wait to spend time with her. They would sit on the couch holding hands and talking for hours. She was always his most ardent and faithful supporter. He took her with him on visitations and to conferences. He pined for her anytime she had to stay behind to tend the home fires. They ministered side by side in church after church until they settled at Grace Baptist in Indianapolis. Jeff loved Margaret more than life. When the children came, no matter how busy, Jeff always made time for the family. Those were hard years, yet great years during which the attendance at Grace Baptist increased from a small crowd to hundreds. The children grew up and their eldest son became Jeff's associate pastor. Thirty years passed in the blink of an eye.

When Jeff announced his retirement, the Grace Baptist congregation surprised Margaret and him with a party. Speechless, the couple stood looking at their smiling faces. These people were their family. He had married them, been there when their children were born, held their hands and prayed with them in difficult times, wept with them at the graves of loved ones and rejoiced at their accomplishments. How could he leave them? He would always be their shepherd. But it was time to pass the mantle to another. Now his son stood at the helm and under his direction the church continued to grow. The people loved him as they had Jeff.

Secretly, Pastor Dillard thought of the passage of Scripture that had plagued him for 40 years: *Jacob have I loved, but Esau have I hated*. Many times Jeff had opened his Bible to that verse and been confounded by it. He puzzled over commentators' explanations of it, gaining no enlightenment. He dared not ask his fellow pastors its meaning. The verse haunted him, because so many times he felt like Esau. This was one of those times.

He compared himself to other pastors who seemed to achieve success with ease and sail through life with no troubles or heartache. Their ministries grew effortlessly. Publishers came to them begging for their writings. TV and radio producers fell all over themselves to offer them contracts. Meanwhile, despite concealing it from everyone including his wife, Jeff struggled in his little corner of the world.

After the evening meal, he told Margaret, "I'm going to walk back over to the church."

"Have a nice walk, dear." Any other evening she would have gone along. Wisely, she knew this was something he had to work out himself. At the kitchen window, she watched her husband amble wearily down the gravel road. As on most evenings, the road was all but deserted. His discouragement notwithstanding, Jeff relished this quiet time. The work for the day done, the hot sun would soon set, leaving the evening cool.

Somewhere in the distance a whippoorwill called to its mate. Jeff approached the neighbor's cattle pasture and smiled at one cow's quest to reach sweeter blades of grass. Stretching her neck under the fence, she reminded him of some church members he had known over the years, jumping from one church to another, never satisfied, believing the grass was greener on the other side and discounting the lush pasture right under their feet.

The coolness of the dusky evening invigorated Jeff. He loved this time of day almost as much as he did the hours he spent with the Lord before daylight. Entering the churchyard, he spotted the paint brush lying where he had tossed it. A murky skin covered the paint in the can. Feeling guilty, he replaced the lid and tapped it onto the bucket. Maybe he could salvage some of what was left. The brush was stiff beyond repair. Pitching it into the trash, he placed the bucket in the storage shed.

Turning his back on the old church building, he walked through the gate to the cemetery. Several Wayside pastors were buried there. "Shepherding this flock is probably what killed them," Jeff said aloud. As soon as the words left his mouth he regretted vocalizing what was in his heart. He looked around to see if someone might have heard. There was no one. The only sound was the mooing of the cows down the road.

One headstone held particular interest for him. According to church records, the man buried there had pastored this church for 25 years. The inscription read, *Jacob Hunter, 1829-1901.* Below were the words *For His Love.*

Pastor Dillard returned to the churchyard. He circled the church, inspecting his handiwork. Sitting on the bench under the oak, he was gripped with a despondency that was jarringly foreign to him. Why am I here? I've worked hard all these years. I looked forward to my retirement. This should be my refuge from the world. He heard the still small voice within: "What of my people?"

"It's not fair, Lord," Jeff said aloud.

"What's not fair, dear?" Margaret appeared out of nowhere, startling him. She sat down beside him.

"I ministered in churches for forty years. Funerals, weddings, hospital visits in the middle of the night and on my day off. Day off–isn't that a joke. I've preached thousands of sermons. Refereed deacons' meetings. Jail ministry, nursing homes. I'm tired. No, scratch that. I'm exhausted. I don't want to be selfish, but will it ever be my time? Our time?"

Taking him by the hand, she said, "Let's go home, dear. Things will look better in the morning."

"I doubt it."

On the walk home, they stopped at the bridge over the creek. The slow running water never failed to soothe him. Earlier on his way from and to the church, he had been too upset to notice. Now he stood with his eyes fixed on a leaf as it made its way lazily under the bridge to appear on the other side. Mentally, Jeff compared himself with that leaf: drifting along with the current with no discernable purpose in life.

The movie Margaret felt sure would perk Jeff up put him to sleep halfway through. She considered waking him but thought better of it. Jeff used to be a ball of energy, waking at 5AM to study and pray until seven, then joining her and the children for breakfast. He often worked until 10 at night and his sermons, powerful and memorable as they were, reflected his efforts.

At 11:30, he roused himself and rose groggily to his feet."Is it over?"

"Yes, but it's okay. We can watch it another time."

After taking his nightly aspirin, Jeff stumbled into the bedroom. Changing into his pajamas, he climbed into bed. Within a few minutes, he was snoring softly.

"You there, get over here!" The harsh voice command startling him. He felt the Roman soldier's lash cut into his shoulder. He knew he was dreaming, yet he could feel the open wound on his back. The man brought the whip down again. Jeff cried out. Before him, a horrifically wounded man lay on the rough cobblestone street. Beaten to a pulp, blood dripped from the man's face and poured off his back. A ring of cruel thorns pierced the top of his head. The massive wooden cross lying on his back seemed to crush him to the ground. Yet it was the man's eyes that struck Jeff. They were clear, peaceful, beautiful, full of love and compassion.

"Take his cross," the soldier ordered, raising his short whip. Stepping forward, Jeff struggled to lift the heavy beams off the fallen man's shoulders.

A gentle smile flitted across Christ lips. "Thank you," He said softly. Tears moistened His eyes. Jeff knew his Savior's tears were not for Himself but for mankind. With herculean effort, Jeff hoisted the cross, bending under it. With its weight pressing on his back, Jeff offered his hand to Christ. Taking it, Jesus struggled to his feet.

Then Jeff was standing with the crowd watching Christ die. He felt stickiness on his hands. Glancing down, he saw they were covered in blood, Christ's blood. The blood He had shed for Jeff's sins.

Jeff's eyes flew open. He looked at the clock: 5:15 AM. Urgency clenched his heart. The office he had created in the spare bedroom had stood idle for the last two months.

Throwing on his robe, he went to it. He cleared off the desk, tossing circulars, ads and junk mail. Going to the kitchen, he brewed a pot of coffee, then returned to his office with a cup of the steaming liquid. Sitting down at the desk, an old, familiar feeling came over him. He was a pastor, a shepherd of the flock. It was his task to lead and guide them through life. He opened his Bible to the account of Christ's ascent to the cross. With tears misting his eyes, Jeff read the scripture with a new attitude. Turning on the computer, he began typing.

Margret woke at 7:45 to find Jeff's side of the bed empty. Hearing the clacking of the keyboard, she walked down the hallway. Looking up from his writing, Jeff smiled at her. Glancing around the neatly organized office, Margaret smiled back.

"Just let me know when breakfast is ready. I'm almost finished here," Jeff said as he had a thousand times before. Returning to his sermon, he heard Margaret in the kitchen humming a familiar hymn. Later that week Jeff turned over his fear of climbing the extension ladder to the Lord and finished painting the church.

On Sunday morning, Jeff stood with his hands gripping the edges of the pulpit and preached with power and authority. His sermon on the eyes of Christ touched the congregation. Several members dabbed at their eyes. Margret smiled. This was the man she had known and loved for the past 45 years. This was her husband and her pastor.

I would like to tell you that under Jeff's leadership the people of Wayside Baptist were galvanized to action. The truth is, however, that the real change took place in the heart of the man of God. From that point on, Jeff Dillard never doubted God's love for him.

Lucille's Library

Lucille loved to read, loved everything about books. She loved the texture of hardback covers, liked the feel of a tome's weightiness in her hands. Turning the pages to discover what was on the other side excited her. The sight of the bold black print on the grainy white paper filled her with a sense of adventure. She appreciated the artful weaving of the story's thread from the first page to the last.

Whether at second-hand shops or yard sales, it was books that caught Lucille's eye. Her favorite haunts were libraries and bookstores. Some of the stores had cozy cafés where she could sit for hours reading the latest best seller. At night, she'd curl up in bed with a book and a cup of hot chocolate in winter or iced tea in the summer.

When reading a mystery or thriller, she would darken the house and read by the light of her small bedside lamp. When the wind was high, she would shiver at the sound of a tree branch brushing against the house. Had the killer escaped the page to lurk outside her bedroom window? Of course not, but such imaginings made the book come to life. Most nights Lucille fell asleep with a book lying open on her chest.

Her collection filled the shelves in her living room and bedroom and overflowed into the kitchen. She cherished every volume, from love stories to mysteries to thrillers. Living alone gave Lucille a different–some might say quirky–perspective on life. Her chosen companions were her books.

For 50 years, Lucille had taught third grade pupils to read. No, she imparted to them more than just reading. She shared her love and respect for the well-turned written phrase. Lucille's greatest pleasure was to see her students' eyes light up as they sailed with Ahab in pursuit of Moby Dick or stood beside Oliver Twist as he begged for more gruel.

Last year at 75, Lucille retired. One stormy summer day, she embarked on a journey she had always dreamed of taking: she began a novel. For years she had anticipated this day. Flitting from one genre to another, she finally settled on making it a mystery.

That late June morning, she took her coffee into the office at the back of her small beach house. A surge of mental energy and excitement made her tingle. Settling herself at the desk, Lucille turned on the computer and opened one of her many notebooks. So many ideas. Which one of them would make a gripping novel? Even though the notebooks were chock full of potential story lines, Lucille jotted down more as they came to her. Some of her musings were inspired by articles in the local newspaper, others by experiences of people she knew. Lucille giggled. Of course she would change the names "to protect the guilty."

Composing the first line with just the right essence to pull in the reader took forever. Should it be straightforward or mysterious? Question or statement? At long last, Lucille rested her fingers on the keyboard and began to type. Her thoughts jerked and sputtered into a paragraph. She re-read it and, dissatisfied, deleted the whole thing.

She worked for three hours, chasing flow and cadence. Sensibility? Maybe it would magically materialize once the story was fully composed. She sat back and read, trying desperately to detect a whiff of intrigue, excitement, anything, in what she had written. Lucille's shoulders slumped. The piece carried no weight, no color, no spark– nothing to compel the reader to turn the page. The budding author knew the hook must be forceful and arouse curiosity. Her words had to inspire her reader to stay with the story to the end.

A dozen times that first day Lucille typed the first few sentences, only to delete them. She sat there trying to unscramble her thoughts while the curser flashed in mocking silence on the idle screen. Why was it so difficult to make this thing flow? She had been reading almost as long as she had been walking. After three days, she finished the first chapter. She read it and asked herself how a reviewer might describe it. The words pedestrian, sophomoric and amateurish came to mind. She purged it and started again.

After struggling with her unwieldy creation for a month, Lucille faced facts. She could not bring the story together. Her hero was a zero, her characters cardboard, her story line preposterous. The more she tried to fix it, the worse the mess became. In the end, she had completed only three pages beyond the first chapter. Reading them over, she couldn't even decipher her own meaning. The words rambled nonsensically, devoid of rhyme or reason. Lucille couldn't kid herself: the fruit of her labor was dead on the vine. It didn't even rise to the level of a hack job.

She closed the word program, tore the pages from the printer and stuffed them into the overflowing wastebasket. Burying her face in her hands, she wept. Shutting down the computer, Lucille felt the sting of reality's bite. She would never be an author. It broke her heart and taught her a lesson. Wordsmithing was a most difficult and demanding venture, only mastered by a special breed and not to be entered into casually. She jammed the notebooks into the drawer of her desk.

Lucille's false start into the world of literature didn't diminish her love for books one iota. If she couldn't write, she would support those who did. To encourage them, she would write and tell them how much she enjoyed their works. No emails, she would send only handwritten letters. At first she wrote to just one author a week. Most didn't reply. Lucille didn't mind. If they answered every fan's letter, they would have no time to write the books she loved to read. When she did receive a response, she would read the letter several times before tucking it neatly into her scrapbook. Some of the authors' letters were written in elegant script on fancy stationary. Others were scribbled on mere scraps of paper. All thanked her for her kind words. She cherished every one.

Within two months, Lucille upped her correspondence campaign to three authors a week, telling them what she enjoyed most about their stories. She never proffered criticism; she would leave that to the reviewers. Her mission was to cheer the authors on in their solitary pursuit. How she envied their ability to craft such skillfully thought-out, ingeniously written tales for people they would never meet—to touch a heart, to change a life.

Reverting to her regular routine, Lucille contented herself with reading and tending her flowers. Having cultivated a thriving rose garden boasting a dozen riotously colorful, fragrant varieties, she placed a wooden bench in its midst. In the early morning or at dusk she would sit there enjoying the blooms' aromas with three or four of her favorite books stacked by her side. As she read, she channeled the protagonist, facing danger, falling in love or becoming the heroine.

One Monday morning, Lucille turned on the news and heard something that sent her reeling. Due to budget constraints, the library's board of directors had voted to close the branch in Lucille's village. Later that day, Lucille did something totally out character: she called her county's main branch to protest. The library director, a pleasant young woman by the name of Sarah, was happy to meet Lucille and speak with her.

Dressed in a business suit for what she considered one of the most important meetings of her life, Lucille arrived at the appointed time and was ushered into Sarah's office. Expressing regret over the board's decision to close the branch, Sarah went on to say they simply had no choice. The building needed thousands of dollars in repairs to bring it up to code. The electrical wiring was ancient; the roof and pipes leaked. The whole place needed a facelift. In addition, lack of funds prevented them from purchasing enough new books to supply the main library and all of its branches. Even if they could, it would be economically inadvisable. Readership in the community had declined. "Our patrons are just not reading books in printed form anymore," Sarah explained. "To keep up with demand we would have to purchase computers. There's no money for that either."

Could anything be done to avoid the closing? No, Sarah said. The books were dated and worn, the peeling paint was exposing the wooden siding to rot, the wiring was a fire hazard, the roof had several major leaks. There was nothing to do but close the library and put the building up for sale.

Crestfallen, Lucille returned home. She poured a glass of iced tea and, picking up her latest purchase, made her way to the back yard. Settled in her favorite spot among the roses, she tried to recapture the excitement she had felt while reading the novel last night. She couldn't concentrate. The thought of losing that little library was unbearable.

Located a block off Main Street, the clapboard building was set back in a peaceful, secluded spot surrounded by a grove of sycamores. At one end of the single room were several comfortable easy chairs arranged in a half circle in front of a working fireplace. A small patch of lawn surrounded the building. Flowerbeds on either side of the front walk had been lovingly tended throughout the years by volunteers, Lucille among them. It would break her heart to see the building abandoned and left to deteriorate.

This library had held a special significance for Lucille since she was a young child. The first time her mother took her there, Lucille's eyes widened with wonder at the tall shelves filled with volumes of every stripe. Over the years, the library became her second home, offering her comfort, learning and enrichment she found nowhere else. Oftentimes on winter days when the snow was falling, she would make her way the few blocks to the quaint building to read of adventure and conquest in distant lands.

The children of the village needed the library.

Lucille closed the book and wiped at the tears misting her eyes. The situation seemed hopeless. She heard the doorbell and glanced at her watch–five after one. The mailman. You could set your clock by Mr. Santos. Rain or snow, summer and winter, his arrival never varied by more than five minutes. As Lucille came around to the front of the house, he waved at her from his departing mail truck. She was sorry she missed him; she had wanted to inquire about his family. His wife suffered from a bad case of arthritis for which the doctor had prescribed a new medication.

Stepping onto the porch, Lucille was delighted to see that her mailbox was full. She took the items back to her bench and sorted them, laying the bills aside. One envelope caught her attention. It was from an author whose name Lucille recognized. His first novel, a Christian thriller, was published several years ago. Lucille had come across a copy of it last summer on a back shelf at a used bookstore.

Dear Lucille,

Thank you for your kind letter. After I wrote Harlan's Pride, *I became very discouraged. When the book was released, slow and meager sales quickly relegated it to the bottom of the heap. Unable to cope with its failure, I quit writing. Two years ago, an accident involving a deer caused my car to flip over. The car was totaled but, thanks to the seatbelt, I was unhurt, though very shaken. That night the Lord brought my propose in life into focus. Since then, I have penned two more novels. Both have struggled to fight their way to the top of the mountain. Happily, my latest,* Erin's Promise, *has reached number 15 on the bestseller list.*

My dear Lucille, it is because of readers like you that this book has risen to the top. Thank you.

Warmest regards,
Gary West

Smiling, Lucille folded the letter and placed it back in the envelope. What a gracious man to attribute his success to her and others who sent him letters of support and encouragement. Returning to her rose garden, she picked up the novel and tried to concentrate. Finding it impossible, she laid it aside, leaned back and closed her eyes. The warmth of the sun and the fragrant, balmy air relaxed her. How could anyone be disheartened on a day like this? Bees hummed around the roses, birds singing their sweet songs flitted about the feeders. And that wonderful letter from Mr. West was such a blessing.

A germ of a "save the library" idea pushed through Lucille's cluttered thoughts. Some of the children she had taught had gone on to start businesses in the area. Her novel and tea forgotten, Lucille hurried into the house. Grabbing the directory off the shelf, she stationed herself at the phone. For the next two hours, she made call after call, pressing buttons until her fingers were sore. With some she got through right away, though most required long waits on hold. During the idle time, she jotted down ideas and figures. Turned down more often than not, Lucille was not deterred. All she needed was a few yeses.

Three days later, plan in hand, Lucille met again with Sarah. The library director was overjoyed. Lucille had done what no one else could.

The following week the branch closed for repairs as local business persons and volunteers descended like worker bees to refurbish the building. A roofing company donated labor and materials to install a new roof. Students from the high school painted the interior under the supervision of their shop teacher. Carpenters built new shelves. Luke's Glass Emporium replaced the glass inlays in the doors and lettered them in gold leaf. Junior High students trimmed the hedges, weeded the flowerbeds and mowed the lawn. An electrician rewired the entire building. New flooring was supplied by the local carpet company. The county highway department repaved the parking lot. The electronics store in a neighboring town contributed five refurbished computers. All gratis.

Early the following week, packages from publishers and authors began arriving with two, sometimes three deliveries a day. Drivers from FedEx, UPS and the postal service stacked boxes of the latest books inside the renovated library.

A retired teacher like Lucille, the current librarian supplemented her income with the stipend she received from the few hours a week the library was open. On days when her duties were light, she and Lucille would reminisce about their days in the classroom. Thrilled to have a hand in the library's rebirth, she and Lucille happily unpacked and cataloged the books until the shelves were full.

Lucille set up a social media crowd-funding account that generated enough to keep the library open for the next year. Gary West was invited to speak at the grand reopening. After his talk, the president of the town council presented the now well-known author with the key to the city.

Afterward, Mr. West held a book signing in the shade of the sycamores. You see, the library was too small to accommodate all in attendance. Over Lucille's objections, Sarah presented her with a plaque commemorating her service. Her dream realized, Lucille returned to her rose garden, where she is happily reading the new novel by her friend Gary West. That is, except on Thursday afternoons, when she conducts story time for the library's newest readers. By the way, Lucille also found her focus, and her new children's book is doing very well.

Author's note

There are thousands of small libraries across America that struggle to provide the latest books and reading materials for their patrons. Lucille's involvement made a difference in her town. Because of folks like her, we enjoy free public libraries in our communities. Next time you visit your local library, take the time to thank those who work there for providing this wonderful service. Perhaps you might even consider volunteering at these places of enjoyment.

A Dog for Sidney

Until she was eight, Sidney Garrett's life was perfect. At least she thought so. Sidney's mother, Marilyn, didn't have to work, so was always there when Sidney came home from school. Under Marilyn's patient guidance, Sidney was learning to cook and keep her room neat, plus help with the household chores.

Once a week mother and daughter would have what they called "girls' night out." They never missed unless the weather was too bad. They would go shopping, eat at a nice restaurant, and go to a movie. At the end of the evening, Sidney's father would greet them at the door and ask about their time together. Then they would all gather in the kitchen for ice cream and to show him Sidney's new outfit. Sidney loved her father, but always cherished those special times with her mother.

Upon arriving home from school a few days after her eighth birthday, Sidney was surprised to see her father's truck in the driveway. As she entered the kitchen, her parents looked dolefully at her. Her mother's eyes were red and puffy. Tears coursed down her father's cheeks. Sidney was sad to see her mother upset, but her father's tears frightened her. She didn't remember ever seeing him cry.

"Sidney, come sit down," her mother said softly. "We have

something to tell you." Sidney's father stood up from his chair and turned away. Arms outstretched, he leaned on the refrigerator and hung his head. Trembling, Sidney took his seat and faced her mother.

Marilyn Garrett took her daughter's hands in hers. "I have never lied or hidden the truth from you and I'm not going to start now." She took a deep breath. "The cancer has spread."

Sidney suddenly felt chilled. She couldn't breathe. Tears sprang from her eyes and ran down her cheeks. "They... they're going to operate, right?"

"No, honey, they can't. It's too late."

"No! No! NO!" Wrenching her hands away, Sidney ran wailing from the kitchen. Racing up the stairs, she ran into her room, slammed the door, threw herself on the bed and sobbed. Her mother, her best friend, was going to die. No hope, no cure. Everything that had been so important just an hour ago now meant nothing. She drifted into a fitful sleep rife with nightmares.

The soft knock on Sidney's door was followed by her mother's gentle voice. "Sidney, honey, dinner's ready." Seeing her standing in the doorway, Sidney tried to burn her mother's image into her mind so she would never forget it. Pushing herself up on her elbows, the tears returned and her voice cracked. "I'm not hungry."

"Oh, honey." Marilyn crossed the room and sat on the edge of the bed. "I know. It's going to be hard for all of us. But God will see us through."

Sidney's breath caught in a fresh rush of tears. She turned

on her back and put her hand over her eyes. "If God's so all powerful why doesn't He heal you?"

Her mother's expression was soft, almost angelic. "I don't know, Sidney. He has a reason and a purpose for each of our lives." She gathered her weeping daughter into her arms. When the tears stopped, they walked arm-in-arm down the stairs.

The next two months were tragic for Sidney. Her mother was either going into the hospital or just coming home. At the beginning of the third month, Marilyn came home for the last time. Never a robust woman, she had lost nearly half her weight.

One afternoon Sidney came home to find a strange woman sitting in the slipper chair beside her mother's bed.

"Hi, sweetheart. This is Mrs. Janis. She's going to be helping us out."

Sidney stared at the woman. Mrs. Janis smiled at her. She stood up and held out her hand. "Hello, Sidney. Your mother has told me a lot about you."

Sidney had known this was coming. Her best friend, Susan, lost her mother two summers ago. She told Sidney these people only showed up at the end. Sidney backed away. "You're from hospice, aren't you?"

"I'm only here to help, honey."

"Don't call me honey. Don't talk to me!" Sidney looked at her mother's pale, shocked face, heard her labored breathing. She couldn't even get out of bed. Her mother was dying and that outburst would probably hasten it.

Ashamed and overwhelmed with grief, Sidney ran from the room. Mrs. Janis didn't follow. She was wise enough to know the girl would have to work this out on her own.

Normally Sidney loved following the animal trails in the woods that bordered her parents' property. Today she wasn't even aware of the creek or the late spring wildflowers. Last year she had gone with her parents to her great aunt's funeral. It was hardly a happy occasion, but she soon forgot it. Now all she could see through the blur of tears was her mother's coffin being lowered into the ground. Sidney wanted to die along with her.

Oblivious to the briar scratches on her legs, she stumbled on and suddenly found herself on the Nobles' property. In the center of the 10-acre tract on the other side of the woods was a two-story farmhouse that had been abandoned for years. Making her way through the overgrown yard, Sidney sat on the front porch steps, crossed her arms over her knees, buried her face and wept.

He heard her from inside as he worked stripping drywall. At 65, this kind of labor was the last thing Vance Turnbull saw himself doing. After 35 years teaching college students, he had been inching toward retirement. Then Gladys developed Alzheimer's. Vance resigned and fought the fight with her, watching over her day and night, lovingly caring for her as she had for him throughout their married life.

She lost the battle last year. Her last days and the funeral were grueling, but Vance stayed by her side to the end. At the funeral home, mourners clasped his hand or patted his back and told him how sorry they were. He held in his sorrow at the cemetery and on the numbingly solitary drive home. That night, sitting in the dark and deathly quiet living room, he dissolved in tears as the weight of losing her came crashing down.

Vance wasn't sorry for Gladys. If there was a shred of joy to be found in his broken heart, it was that she was with the Lord. She was enjoying her new life in heaven, untouched by the disease that took her life. It occurred to Vance that he had lost the real Gladys long ago. When his weeping finally ended, he felt cleansed.

Over the next few months, it became clear to Vance that he could stay in their house no longer. He lived there with Gladys for 40 years, and she still inhabited every inch it. At first Vance found comfort in her ubiquitous presence, but as time wore on it grew steadily more depressing. Giving away the hospital bed didn't help. Sleeping in the guest room only deepened his sorrow. There was nothing to do but move.

The house sold quickly. Wherever Vance went from there, it had to be in the country. He didn't care what the place looked like. One evening during an internet search, he came across the farmhouse. He called the realtor the next morning. Yes, it was still available. Vance drove the hundred miles to see it. The house was in much worse shape than the photos in the ad depicted. The realtor explained that the pictures were taken two years earlier, right after the foreclosure.

Always the visionary, Vance saw the farmhouse for what it could be, not how it was. Estimating the cost of repairs and improvements, he made an offer far below what the bank was asking. They countered with one he could manage. Two weeks later, he moved in and began renovating. He cleaned out the master bedroom first, enough for it to be habitable. He set up a card table in the spare bedroom on which to place the coffeepot, hotplate and microwave. On the third night, he dedicated the house to the Lord and the memory of his beloved Gladys. Although Vance's grief eased as the days and weeks passed, his dear wife lived on in his dreams. He wouldn't have had it any other way.

Pulling down the stained drywall in the kitchen, Vance heard something and paused. Stepping to the window, he saw a little girl sitting on his back steps. She appeared to about eight or nine. Her blond hair was in a pigtail. She was crying. Not wanting to frighten her, Vance opened the door just a crack. Pushing his nose into the opening, Ramie forced his way out.

Sidney felt something warm and wet on her cheek. Startled, she raised her head and stared into Vance's Sheltie's soft brown eyes while the dog lapped at her tears with his scratchy tongue. "That's Ramie," a gravelly voice behind her said. "He can't stand to see a lady cry."

Sidney jumped up and brushed off the seat of her pants. "I'm… sorry," she said, more embarrassed than frightened. "I didn't know anyone lived here."

Vance stepped out. Leaning on his cane, he eased down onto the wooden step. Ramie snuggled up against the elderly man, who wrapped his arm around the grinning dog. His tongue lolling to the side, Ramie kept his eyes on Sidney.

Patting the dog, Vance gave the girl a sympathetic smile. "I just moved here last week." Sidney's eyes brightened a bit as she studied the old man. With his smile crinkling his face, his whitish-gray hair and slightly sad brown eyes, he looked like a kindly grandfather. "I've been so busy I haven't had time to meet my neighbors." Vance held out his hand to receive Sidney's one solemn shake. "My name is Vance and you've met Ramie."

At the sound of his name, the dog jumped to his feet and went to the girl, wagging his tail and nuzzling her arm. Sidney let out a little giggle and rubbed his head. "I wish I had a dog," she said wistfully. "We had one, but he died last summer. He was already old when I was born." Her eyes welled up again.

"It's hard to lose someone or something you love," Vance said. "Ramie has been with me for six months now. He's good to have around. Keeps me from getting too lonesome."

"Don't you have any family?" Sidney asked with childlike forthrightness.

"Ramie is my family now," Vance answered, his face creased with sadness.

"Where's your wife?" Sidney pressed, then wished she hadn't as tears sprang to the elderly man's eyes.

"She went to heaven."

"My mom's going to heaven," Sidney said, wiping the tears from her cheeks. "I wish she wouldn't." With a loud sob, she bolted from the steps and ran into the woods. Hesitating only slightly, Ramie started to follow.

"Ramie! No, boy," Vance said sharply. "She needs to be alone now." He stared for a few moments at the tree line through which Sidney had fled, then took the dog inside and returned to his work.

Picking up the hammer, Vance swung it viciously at the drywall. "Ooooh, I hate you, Death," he shouted as he yanked the claw through the crumbling sheetrock. "You take a loving wife and a little girl's mother. You have no heart, no pity." He swung the hammer again, obliterating what was left of the wall. He would feel it in the morning, but right now he didn't care.

Halfway home, Sidney dropped onto a decaying log and wept until she had no more tears. She felt helpless. What could she do? "Go home." She loved her mother; she would not let her go through this alone. As she came near the house, she saw a light in her mother's bedroom. Straightening her shoulders and forcing braveness onto her face, Sidney entered the house.

Vance's mind whirled with the memory of that last night at the hospital when Gladys breathed her last. With tears streaming endlessly down his face, he had held her hand, leaned over her and whispered, "I love, I love you, I love you." The anguish of her funeral and burial came rushing back. He shuddered as his impulse to crawl into the casket and be buried with her overwhelmed him as it had that day. From out of nowhere came the same crushing loneliness that had followed him out of the cemetery.

Back at home, he wandered through the rooms, feeling both comforted by and fearful of Gladys's inescapable presence. It was there in the knick-knacks she collected over the years. In the closet full of her clothes. He took the items she loved and stored them away. He emptied the closets and drawers and gave everything to Goodwill.

With those last heartrending acts, he said a tearful goodbye to his Gladys. Now he would finish out his life as close to heaven as the little village of Barker, New York, could get him. This old farmhouse had seemed to beckon to him. Now he worked to make it his own.

Late that night, Vance stirred and laid his hand on the other side of the bed. She wasn't there. He was glad he was alone so no one could see his tears. Roused from his sleep, Ramie whined and laid his head on Vance's knee. Rumpling the dog's coat, Vance whispered, "I'm never alone as long as you're around."

Switching off the radio beside the bed, Vance listened to the wind rustling through the trees. What a change from the city with its constant din of traffic and sirens. A stiff breeze blew through the open window, rattling the blinds. Rain was coming. That was fine with Vance. The roof on this house was sound, less than five years old. Getting up to close the window, Vance caught a glimpse of light through the swaying trees from what he thought must be Sidney's house. He sighed. "Lord, be with her. Show me a way to comfort her and her family."

Back in bed, Vance turned on his side and closed his eyes. Ramie circled a few times before lying down against Vance's back. Reaching around to pat him, the elderly widower whispered sleepily, "Thank you for being my friend."

The next morning as he tore away the drywall in the living room, Vance stopped in mid-swing. He looked at Ramie, who was lying across the doorway threshold watching him work. Now almost fully grown, the pup had been such a blessing to Vance. After Gladys, Ramie was Vance's best friend. When it became apparent that Gladys was dying, the dog would lie next to Vance each time he knelt in prayer. The night after the funeral as he sat weeping in the living room, Vance could have sworn he saw tears in Ramie's eyes.

"A puppy, that's what Sidney needs," Vance told his friend.
Ramie raised up on his haunches and cocked his head. "Not
a grown dog like you, but a puppy that can grow with her
and comfort her in her sorrow." Ramie let out a little yip of
agreement, bringing a smile to Vance's lips. "Yup, that's
what she needs." How to convince the girl's parents of that,
Vance wasn't sure. "I don't even know them," he said with
a sigh.

Vance worked through the day, taking frequent breaks. By
evening, the house was ready for the contractors. The place
looked like a bomb hit it. Down to the studs, the morass of
exposed wires, vents, two-by-fours and pipes presented a
starkly uncomely appearance. The hardwood floors would
be striking only after the old paint was removed and several
coats of varnish applied. Vance shook his head. Why
anyone would paint beautiful oak flooring battleship gray
was beyond him.

After a supper of soup and a sandwich, Vance settled down
to find a contractor. His first two calls went unanswered.
Finally on the third, the man thanked him for considering
his company, but explained it would be two to three months
before he could get to the job. "I'm sorry, where did you
say you live?"

"Out on Old Post Road," Vance answered. "Don't know
why it's called that."

The man chuckled. "Years ago there was a little old shack
of a post office where the 7-Eleven is now. Been gone for
decades but I guess someone thought to name the road after
it. Say, listen, there's a guy who lives near you. Name's
Rick Garrett. He's honest and does good work. You might

be able to get him. May not be able to put in full days, though."

"Why is that?" Vance asked, pretty sure he knew the answer.

"His wife has cancer. Last I heard they were going to bring in hospice. She hasn't got long."

Vance thanked the man and ended the call. He hesitated to call Sidney's father. Just imagining the family's misery ripped open his heart again. He thought of Gladys's expenses from the doctors and hospital. Though their insurance paid most of the cost, he still ended up with a hefty bill. If he hadn't saved for both of their final expenses, he would have really been hurting.

Punching in the number, Vance waited. By the fifth ring he was about to hit the end button. "Garrett Construction," a man's voice said. "How can I help you?"

"Yes, Mr. Garrett, this is Vance Turnbull. I purchased the farmhouse just down the road from you. I've completed the demo on the downstairs but I'm afraid I've reached the limit of my expertise."

"Yes. I saw that someone bought the place. It's a good, solid piece of property."

"You know the house then?"

"Sure. As you probably know, the house was vacant for years. But it's structurally sound with a good roof, and the siding is less than ten years old."

"That's what I understood from the realtor. It's the interior that's a mess. It looks like someone turned a whirling dervish loose inside it."

Garret laughed. "Well, Mr. Turnbull, I'd like to help you. But I'm not taking on any long-term projects right now."

"I understand. One of the other contractors I spoke with explained your situation. I lost my wife just recently."

"Then you know what my family is going through," Rick Garrett said, his voice tinged with sadness.

"To a certain extent. My wife had Alzheimer's. She wasn't aware of what was going on around her for a long time."

"I'm sorry. That must have been very difficult for both of you."

"It was. However, she's in heaven now, free of the disease. Mr. Garrett–"

"Call me Rick, please."

"Rick, forgive me for being forward. But I know how medical expenses can eat up your income. Because of the proximity of our homes, I'd like to propose that you work on your own schedule. When you need to be with your wife and family, there won't be any problem on my part with the delay. In other words, work when you can. Whether it's for an hour or five, I'd be very grateful."

"That's very kind of you, Mr. Turnbull."

"Vance."

"Vance. Can you give me a day to think about it?"

"Of course."

"Thank you. I'll call you around this time tomorrow. Good night, sir."

Sidney spent every spare minute with her mother. She became Mrs. Janis's best helper. As Marilyn grew weaker, Sidney helped feed her, assisted with changing her bedding, read to her and prayed with her.

After talking it over with Marilyn, Rick decided to take Vance's job. The first day he worked for two hours, taking only a short break to drive home and check on his wife. One morning in June, Rick left on a home check and didn't return. Later that day he called to tell Vance that Marilyn was gone. She passed away just before noon with Rick and Sidney by her side. Rick would return to work the following week. Vance told him to take as much time as he needed and assured him of his prayers. Promising to inform him of the funeral arrangements, Rick ended the call.

Picturing the heart-broken little girl, Vance kneeled, wept and prayed for her and her father. It had been hard enough to lose his wife. How much more difficult it must be to lose a parent. At his side, Ramie placed his paw on Vance's arm and whimpered. Hugging the dog, the elderly man sobbed into his fur.

The funeral was somber, yet peaceful. The pastor spoke of Sidney's mother's love for her husband, her daughter and her church. She was devoted to the Lord, he said, and always cheerfully willing to help others. "Heaven is sweeter because of this dear woman," he said as he closed the service. Except for dropping off the meals he bought at the restaurant for them, Vance left the family alone. They needed time to grieve without interference.

A week later, Rick arrived at the farmhouse with Sidney in tow. As he and Vance spoke, she played with Ramie. "I can start on the upstairs tomorrow. That's the soonest I can get someone to watch Sidney," Rick said as he watched his daughter throwing a ball for the dog to fetch.

"Why don't you bring her along? Ramie could use the exercise. And she can bring some toys in case she gets tired of playing with him."

"You're sure it won't be an inconvenience?" Rick asked, although he looked relieved.

"If there's anything this old house needs it's a child playing on the front lawn," Vance said, his face crinkling with a smile.

The following afternoon right after school, Rick pulled alongside the farmhouse with a small trailer hitched to his pickup. As soon as Sidney's foot hit the ground, Ramie bounded out to greet her. As Vance and Rick worked, she played ball with the dog, served him imaginary tea, and decked out a very tolerant Ramie in one of her old dresses. As work wrapped up for the day, Vance broached the subject with Rick. "I don't know what I would have done without that dog. He was such a comfort to me when I lost Gladys."

"This has been one of the most difficult times I've ever gone through," Rick said as he joined Vance at the window. Below them, Sidney's laughter rang out as she ran in circles with Ramie right behind her. Vance could sense Rick stiffening when she abruptly stopped, knelt on the ground and opened her arms, catching the dog in them and hugging his neck. The men could hear her sobs.

"She does that quite a bit," Rick said sadly. "She'll be playing or doing something else and she'll just suddenly start crying."

"It will probably go on for a while," Vance said. "You know, Rick, dogs are great comforters of sorrow."

For the next hour, the two men worked in silence. At five, they went looking for Sidney and the dog and found them curled up on the back porch, asleep.

"I hate to wake her. She looks so peaceful. She doesn't sleep well since…" Rick's words trailed off.

"I have a friend whose dog, Ramie's mother, had a litter about six months ago. In fact, that's how I got Ramie. I spoke with the guy yesterday. He has one pup left," Vance said.

"Vance, I appreciate that. But between the hospital bills and the funeral I just can't afford to buy a dog right now." Ramie stirred and pushed himself up on his haunches. Wagging his tail, he appeared to be smiling.

Vance spoke softly so as not wake the sleeping child. "Rick, from what I've seen, you do excellent work. Your prices are reasonable. When you're finished with the house I want to give you a bonus. But I'd like you to have part of it now. Will you let me give Sidney that puppy?"

Rick's eyes rested on his daughter as he thought. "She loved old Ollie. Sure would be great to have another dog around. She needs a good companion."

"Wonderful. But please don't say anything to her just yet. He may have already sold the pup."

Nodding, Rick went to the sleeping girl and picked her up. Stirring, Sidney wrapped her arms around her father's neck. "I dreamed about Mommy," she murmured against his cheek. "She had on a white robe. She was smiling. She said she loves us and misses us."

"We miss her too, sweetheart." Carrying her to the truck, Rick turned to Vance. "Thank you, my friend. Let me know what you find out."

Three days later, the two men were working in the living room when a pickup pulled into the driveway. The sign on its side read:

Drew's Kennels

Excitedly distracted from playing with Ramie, Sidney dropped the ball and ran toward the lanky man as he stepped out of the truck. Overjoyed at the sight of his old friend, Ramie made a mad dash around her. Dropping to one knee, the man ruffled Ramie's ears, laughing as the dog yipped and licked his face. Smiling and chuckling, Rick and Vance watched from the porch.

"You must be Sidney," the man said. "I wasn't sure if my old buddy would remember me. Looks like he does, huh?"

"He's my friend too."

"Yes, I know. My name is Drew. Your dad asked me to bring you a gift." Straightening up, Drew opened the passenger door and reached in. "Come on. It's okay." He turned and watched Sidney's eyes and grin widen as he held out the wriggling puppy. He set the dog on the ground. After taking a few tentative steps, the pup looked back. "Go on," Drew said with a wave of his hand.

Kneeling, Sidney opened her arms wide. "Come on boy, come to me." With an eager "rolf, rolf," the pup bounded into her arms. Within minutes, Sidney and the two dogs were happily at play.

Rick and Vance grinned at each other. Drew joined them on the porch. "Rick, I'd like you to meet Drew Pierson." The two men shook hands. "Drew bravely suffered through two of my classes. Drew, Rick's helping me rebuild what I tore up."

"Thanks for bringing the pup," Rick said. "He's exactly what she needed. As I'm sure Vance told you, she just lost her mother."

"Yes, he did. I'm so sorry," Drew said softly.

"Let me get my checkbook," Vance said.

As Vance turned toward the door, Drew caught his arm. "No, I can't let you do that. Rick, when Vance told me about Sidney, I knew this dog would be perfect for her. The mother dog died three weeks ago. The pup's been lost without her."

"God answered my prayer even before I asked Him," Vance said.

"Mine too," Rick said.

Sidney tossed the ball between the two dogs. Ramie started

for it, then dropped to the ground on his belly. The pup saw his chance. Chasing it down and grabbing it in his mouth, he proudly carried it back to his new mistress and dropped it at her feet. Watching from heaven, Sidney's mother smiled.

The Mission Bored

Faith Madison sighed as she loaded the dinner plates and silverware into the dishwasher. "I really don't want to go."

"Then don't," Gilbert said. He sat down at the kitchen table with a second cup of coffee and spread out the newspaper before him.

"If I don't Maggie and Amy will be by themselves," Faith said. She plunked down in the chair across from her husband and stared into her coffee cup. In just a few minutes she would have to leave for church.

Gilbert looked up from his paper with knitted brows. "Honey, is it really that bad?" As a youth pastor, he had always been encouraged by Faith's also being involved in an aspect of the ministry. Until now.

"You have no idea, Gil. We pass around the same old snacks, discuss the same old topics and work on the same projects that seem to never get done. We start and end with the girls saying the same old tired prayers. I'm not sure God is even listening anymore." Faith omitted the fact that at every third meeting it was she who led in prayer.

"What about reading the missionary's letters?" Gilbert asked, trying to be helpful.

"Huh? Uh, no. No way, not since that horrible letter from the Morris's last year. You could almost hear that poor woman screaming off the page." Faith shuttered. She could still see the photo of the native mother holding her dead baby boy. For three weeks afterward, whenever Faith closed her eyes all she could see was that poor little child's body.

Gilbert came around the table and kissed his wife. "I'm sure you'll think of something to liven up the group."

"I hope so. Thursday night is the most boring night of the week," she said, returning his kiss carefully so as not to mess up her hair and makeup.

Waving to Gilbert as he stood in the doorway, Faith started the car and bowed her head. "Lord, please make something exciting happen tonight so we don't have to sit through the same old boring meeting." A wry smile crossed her face as she backed out of the driveway. Maybe the Lord will do something to make shy little Amy come out of her shell.

At Christ Church, she parked next to Amy's Ford compact. Great. Maggie was late. Maybe she wasn't coming. With two small children, Maggie would always arrive late or, if her husband was out of town, not at all. Faith frowned. A meeting with just her and Amy? Now that would really be boring. Faith would have to be the one to initiate and sustain any interaction between them. She thought of calling Amy from the parking lot and begging off. No, it wasn't right to reject Amy because of her upbringing.

Reluctantly, Faith opened the door to the darkened hallway. The only illumination came from the light under the stove hood in the tiny kitchen. The walk down the hall felt creepy. Stepping into the fellowship hall, she hesitated. In the dim light she saw two silhouettes, one towering over the second, smaller figure that was hunched on the floor. Faith switched on the lights. "Why you are in the dark? Are we trying to save on—"

The smile died on her face. Amy, her face tear-soaked and ghostly white, was curled up almost in a ball. A frail, slight woman, she looked as though she was trying to disappear. A haggard-looking, raw-boned young man stood over her. To Faith the pistol in his hand looked as big as a canon.

Terror shot through her. She felt weak. The man wheeled around and gave her a steely-eyed, menacing look. She grasped the wall for support. "Come in, sit down and shut up," he said hoarsely, gesturing with the gun. Grabbing Amy by the arm, he hauled her up and plopped her onto the seat of a metal folding chair. Amy raised her terrified face and looked pleadingly at Faith. Her thick glasses made her wide eyes look like saucers.

Always timid, Amy had just recently begun coming out of her shell. At their last meeting, she haltingly read a poem about loneliness that she had written. With one swipe this man, whoever he was, spooked that all away. The thought made Faith angry. She stumbled on trembling legs to the closest chair.

"Not there," he growled. "Next to your friend." Scared witless, Faith pushed herself up and, holding onto the row of tables, staggered the short distance. Dropping into the chair next to Amy, she reached for the young woman's hand. Amy's ice cold fingers squeezed so hard Faith gasped with pain.

"Empty your purses on the table," the man demanded. Faith mustered the courage to look at his face. He was just a boy, surely not a day over 18. The uneven stubble peppering his cheeks and chin did little to camouflage his acne. His eyes were red and watery and he kept wiping his nose. He's high on something, Faith thought. Just this morning she'd read an article in the paper about drug use among teenagers and the crimes they committed to feed their habits. "Better to lose your money than your life," the writer had warned. She resolved to do whatever it took for her and Amy to survive.

With her hands shaking, Amy upended her purse over the table top. A tube of Chap Stick and a small bottle of cheap perfume bounced to the floor. Some singles tumbled out. Shifting the pistol to his left hand, the man sorted through the tissues, keys and other objects. He grasped a handful of crumpled bills. Counting them, he shouted, "Eight dollars? That all you got?" He leaned down until his nose nearly touched Amy's. "You better come up with somethin' better than this." He threw the bills in her face.

With his attention turned from her, Faith reached into her purse. Jerking out the can of pepper spray Gilbert insisted she carry, she yelled, "Hey!"

Still leaning over Amy, the boy turned to gawk in Faith's direction. He opened his mouth. "Wha–?" She hit him with a full load square in the eyes and mouth. Screaming, he dropped the gun and fell to his knees. Yelping, he tore at his face as he writhed on the floor.

"Amy, run! Run!" Faith screamed. White with fear, Amy nonetheless had the presence of mind to grab her cell phone. She dashed out of the fellowship hall like a runner crossing the finish line. With the man disabled, Faith kicked the gun out of his reach. She backed up a few paces, ready to hose him again should it prove necessary. Faith could hear Amy blubbering in near hysteria in what Faith thought must be the pastor's office.

"There's a man with a gun at Christ Church. He's going to kill us!" There was a pause. "Wickham Avenue. I don't know the number. Look it up! What? Don't tell me to calm down! We need help. NOW!" Her trembling voice echoed down the hallway.

Snatching up the gun, Faith backed up a safe distance. On his knees now, the man whined, "Why did you do that?" He grasped the edge of the nearest table to pull himself to his feet.

"Stay right there. Don't you move," Faith croaked. Knowing she sounded like a weak kitten, she waved the gun at him. She didn't think she had it in her to shoot him. But she would surely give him another shot of pepper spray if he tried anything.

"I wasn't going to hurt you," he whimpered, rubbing his eyes with one hand while clinging onto the back of a chair with the other.

"You held a gun on us. You were going to kill us."

"It's just a toy. I just wanted to scare you. Can I please get some water? My eyes are burning out of my head."

Watching for any aggressive move, Faith backed into the kitchen and filled a glass with water. Keeping her distance, she set it on the table two feet from the boy's hand. "On the table to your left," she said. Moaning, he grabbed the glass and upended it into his eyes. Sirens were approaching. Emboldened, Faith piped up, "You wanted money for drugs, didn't you?"

"No. I was hungry," he simpered unconvincingly.

Faith bristled as he pulled out the chair and collapsed into it. "Don't lie to me, young man."

Still trying to clear his eyes, he blinked in the direction of her voice while pawing at them with the hem of his T-shirt. "Okay, okay. I was looking for a fix. Can I just go now? You can have the gun."

"Oh, no, my friend. You stay right where you are." She aimed the can at his face and kept her finger on the button. There was commotion at the side door of the church.

"This way!" Amy shouted. She charged into the fellowship hall, her eyes bugging out. As she slid to a halt the two police officers following behind nearly knocked her down. They pointed their weapons at the young man in the chair. Faith laid the pistol on a table out of his reach.

"Please stand to the side," the lead officer said, motioning Amy out of the way. "We'll take it from here."

Faith lowered the can of pepper spray and set it beside the gun. Her sense of relief was quickly interrupted by the sharp pain in her arm and her aching hand.

"Get on your face now, Robbie," one of the officers commanded.

"I didn't do nothing," the boy whined as he stretched out on the floor.

The officers holstered their side arms. "Hands behind your back." Meeting no resistance, the officer snapped on the cuffs.

"He had a gun," Faith said, pointing at it.

"Lady, I told you, it's a toy," the boy sputtered. Tears still leaked from his swollen, red eyes.

"Yeah, we know. He's done this before. We're old friends aren't we, Robbie?" The cop patted the boy on the shoulder. "You know, one of these days we're gonna be calling the coroner for you. Somebody' going to shoot you thinking that toy is real."

The two officers hoisted Robbie to his feet and propelled him toward the exit. "We'll need you to come down to the station to press charges," one of them called over his shoulder to the women.

Spent and feeling weak, Faith dropped into a chair. "You mean now, tonight?"

"Tomorrow morning will be fine," the cop answered loudly. "Robbie's not going anywhere. By the way, his last name is Walters." Then they were gone, shoving the boy before them through the door.

Amy collapsed in a chair and began bawling big, hulking sobs that shook her body. Faith took the younger woman in her arms and patted her on the back. "Amy, Amy, shh. It's all right now. He's gone and he's not coming back."

Amy drew back. Faith saw the terror still in her eyes. "I was so scared, Faith."

"I know. So was I. But it's over now."

"No, it's not. We'll have to see him again in court. I'm not sure I can do that." Amy drew a shuttering breath. "You... you were wonderful. The way you stood up to him and held him off? I couldn't have done it."

She chattered on. Faith was only half listening, thinking that if Amy didn't quit babbling she would run screaming from the church. Instead, she said, "Come on, let's get you home. Are you okay to drive or should I drop you at your apartment?"

Amy sniffled and dabbed at her eyes. "I… I'll be all right. I have to be at the library early. We have a box of James Patterson's new book in the storage room that I need to catalog." Her eyes shined as they always did when she spoke about books.

Faith walked Amy to her car. Sliding behind the wheel, Amy glanced up at Faith's questioning look. "Don't worry about me, Faith. I'm going home and right to bed. Although I do think I'm going to swear off reading thrillers and mysteries for a while."

Watching her drive away, Faith said a prayer for the woman who she knew saw her as a mother figure. Having grown up an orphanage, was it any wonder poor Amy was so frightened of life and insecure? Faith would ask Gil about setting up some counseling sessions for her.

Sitting in her car, Faith leaned her forehead against the wheel and sobbed. A few minutes later, she dried her tears and drove home. She couldn't get the image of that boy out of her mind. Was he so desperate for drugs he would barge into a church and try to rob them with a toy gun? God forbid if that thing had been real. The prospect shook her so badly she nearly ran a stop light. Turning into her driveway, she let the car coast the last few feet. Switching off the engine, she took her cell phone from her purse. Punching in Amy's number, she counted the number of rings.

"Oh, it's you Faith. I had a crazy thought that guy might be calling me from jail." Amy's attempt at laughter sounded more like a sob.

"I just wanted to make sure you got home all right. Good night, Amy."

Hearing Faith's key in the lock, Gilbert met her in the

kitchen. Seeing her broken expression, his smile collapsed. "What's wrong? Don't tell me somebody didn't show up."

"Oh, Gil." Faith threw herself into her husband's arms.

When her sobbing slowed he guided her to a chair. After pouring her a cup of tea, he sat down beside her and spoke softly. "What happened?" He listened quietly, interrupting with questions only twice.

"So Amy and I have to go down to the police station in the morning."

"What's the kid's name?"

"The policeman said Robbie Walters."

"And the gun was a toy?"

"Yes, thank God. But it looked real enough."

"I think he just wanted to scare you. Like you said, he was just looking for drug money. I'm glad you kept your wits about you."

Faith chuckled. "Amy screamed into her phone so loud she must have broken the dispatcher's ear drum."

Gil laughed and put his arm around her. "Thank the good Lord you're safe. Let's get some sleep. Things will look better in the morning." They didn't.

Faith slept in fits and starts. Every time she closed her eyes she saw the pimply-faced boy brandishing that gun. She finally drifted off around two, only to snap awake a few hours later, trembling from a nightmare she couldn't remember.

She went into the kitchen and turned on the stove light. The headache she'd tried all night to ignore hit full bore. While waiting for the coffee a terrifying thought shot through her. Were all the doors locked? What about the windows? Gulping down two aspirins with the steaming coffee, she winced when it burned her tongue and went to check. Locked and bolted, all.

Back in the kitchen, she laid her Bible on the table and opened it randomly. *I was in prison and ye came unto me.* She grasped a sheaf of pages and flipped them. Running her finger down the page, she stopped to read Isaiah 61:1.

When Faith was three, she started wondering and asking about God. At six, she received Christ as her Savior. Over the years, she had sung in the choir, taught Sunday school, taken part in the nursing home ministry and gone with Gil twice to the rescue mission. Faith was no shrinking violet when it came to soul-winning. The thought of going into a jail and dealing with criminals, however, was daunting.

She was still pondering the idea when Gil stepped into the kitchen. He poured a cup of coffee and sat down. "I was trying to think where I heard that Walters boy's name before." He sipped the steaming liquid and grimaced. "More sugar." Scooping in a second spoonful, he continued. "About a year ago a woman was killed by a drunk driver. I read in the paper that her son sat by her grave for three days until they finally dragged him away. His name was Robbie."

Faith's shoulders sagged. She looked at her husband and sighed. "His mother?"

"That's what I'm thinking. I'll look up her obituary

online." He left and was back several minutes later. "I talked to Brownie at the sheriff's office. He said the kid's been in and out of trouble since his mother was killed. Evidently he turned to opioids to deal with the pain."

"So it's the same boy?"

"Yeah. Brownie says he was never in trouble before that. No juvenile record, not even a traffic violation."

"Amy and I are supposed to go down and press charges. I'm not so sure I can."

"Well, he did hold a gun on you," Gil reminded her. "You had no way of knowing it wasn't real. Next time he might mess with someone who'll shoot him believing it is."

"Do you think I should try to help him?"

"He has to be dealt with, honey. You'll have to decide if his going to prison is the way to do it."

"I know he needs the Lord."

"Yes, and a lot of people have found the Lord in prison." He patted her arm. "I have to go. I know you'll do the right thing."

Faith thought of their daughter, Ruth. She was attending her first semester in college and Faith missed her terribly. Gil had tried to fill the gap by spending more time with Faith, even suffering in silence on a few shopping trips to the mall with her. Mother and daughter spoke by phone every few days and exchanged emails regularly. Still, it wasn't the same as being face to face. Now as Faith sat with her head in her hands, Gil sensed her maternal instincts kicking in.

"It was just a toy," Faith reasoned. "I'm going to call Amy."

"Will she be up?"

"What?" Gil's voice startled her. She thought he had left.

"Oh, Gil, I'm sorry. I was so wrapped up I didn't even think about breakfast."

Gil chuckled. "It's okay. I have a men's prayer breakfast this morning. I gotta get going. I love you." He kissed her. "Call you later."

"I love you too," Faith said. "Thank you for being there for me."

When Amy heard what Faith had in mind the phone went silent. "Amy, are you there?"

"Yes. Look, Faith, I know what the Bible says about visiting jails and forgiveness and all that. But I don't think I'll ever walk into Christ Church again without jumping at shadows." Her voice trembled. "That front door was left unlocked. He was hiding in the fellowship hall. I practically bumped into him when I went in there. I wanted to warn you, but he said if I made a sound he'd kill me."

"I don't think he meant to harm us. He was being driven by his addiction."

""Maybe so, but we couldn't know that. I'm sorry, Faith, I can't go along with it. I'm definitely filing charges."

"Amy, did you know that he's an orphan? His mother was killed by a drunk driver last year." There was silence.

"Amy, are you there?"

"That's no excuse for what he did," Amy answered harshly. Faith couldn't help but notice how brave and assertive the otherwise meek little woman could be over the telephone. "I have to go," Amy told her. The phone went dead.

At eight o'clock Pastor Mike Dunlin called. "Faith, I just heard what happened last night. I'm so sorry. I locked up the church at twenty after seven, right after the deacons' meeting. He must have jimmied the lock."

Faith recounted the events of the night before. "It was pretty scary, Pastor."

"They told me you held him off until the police got there. That's incredible, Faith. Listen, I'd understand if you ladies want to disband the women's missionary society."

"I have a different idea," Faith said. Over the next few minutes, she outlined her plan. Drawing a deep breath, she waited for her pastor's reaction, growing tense when he hesitated.

"Faith, I've known you for four years. You and Gil are great assets to the church. You've taught Sunday school, sung in the choir and helped tremendously with all the activities. If I had a hundred members like you and Gil, the glory of God would shine like a beacon that the folks in this town and every town around it would clearly see."

Faith face flamed. Praise always made her self-conscious and uncomfortable. She had no idea how to respond. She opened her mouth but the pastor's voice stopped her. "Nope, nope, now you know I'm speaking the truth. I won't try to change your mind, but I will ask, do you know what you're getting yourself into?"

"Uh, I–"

"Inmates aren't like children in a Sunday School class. Granted, a few just got caught up in the system, but the majority of them are hardened criminals."

Discouragement clouded Faith's face. "Are you saying this is a bad idea?"

"No, Faith, it's a great idea. But you should take someone with you has experience dealing with this type of person. Let me make some calls."

"Thank you, Pastor." As soon as Faith pressed the end button, doubt assailed her. She pictured herself battered and bloody on the floor of a grimy jail cell. Her coffee cup tumbled from her hand. She grabbed the sponge to sop up the mess before it could wend its way under the stove. The phone rang. "Hello?"

"Hello, Mrs. Madison? This is Phil Sanders. Your pastor called me and said you might be interested in working with our organization."

"Who are you again, sir?"

"I'm sorry. I was under the impression you wanted to help out in the jail ministry."

"I... I don't know. I was thinking about it. Is it safe?"

"These days it's probably safer than walking down the street. Don't get me wrong. When you're working with these people things can go wrong very quickly. But Christ dealt with the worst of society. Remember, Faith, He died between two thieves who were put to death because of their crimes."

On Tuesday night Faith and Gil met Phil Sanders outside the security complex. A friendly correctional officer escorted them into an empty room. Faith clutched Gil's hand. Her palms were damp and she had the urge to run. "Do they lock the door?" she asked Sanders.

"Yes, but I have a radio in case there's trouble." Sanders smiled at her. "Don't worry, everything will be fine."

Faith's grip made Gil's fingers ache. She prayed, silently and nervously. "Lord, are you sure about this?"

The door opened and about 20 men filed in. Most of them smiled and shook hands with Sanders. When Robbie Walters entered, Faith's heart nearly stopped. Keeping his eyes down, he slipped into the last seat in the back row.

"Let's pray," Sanders said. All the men, including Robbie, bowed their heads. After a brief prayer, Sanders announced, "We have two special guests with us tonight. Gil is the youth pastor at Christ Church and Faith is his wife." At the name of the church, Robbie raised his head and locked eyes with Faith. He quickly looked down but she could see his face crumbling. She let go of Gil's hand.

"I have it on good authority that Faith is an excellent singer," Sanders said. He turned to her. "Would you bless us with a song?"

"Of course," Faith answered softly. Thinking of what song would be appropriate, she stood.

Does Jesus care when my heart is pained
Too deeply for mirth or song,

As the burdens press, and the cares distress,
And the way grows weary and long?

Oh, yes, He cares, I know He cares,
His heart is touched with my grief;
When the days are weary, the long nights dreary,
I know my Savior cares.

Does Jesus care when my way is dark
With a nameless dread and fear?
As the daylight fades into deep night shades,
Does He care enough to be near?

Does Jesus care when I've tried and failed
To resist some temptation strong;
When for my deep grief there is no relief,
Though my tears flow all the night long?

Does Jesus care when I've said "goodbye"
To the dearest on earth to me,
And my sad heart aches till it nearly breaks—
Is it naught to Him? Does He see?

Trembling at first, Faith's voice smoothed out until her tones echoed sweetly down the hallway into the cells of the inmates who passed on the Bible study. Gil stood in the corner smiling as he watched the woman he loved minister to these forgotten men.

Several lives were changed that night. Robbie Walters and three others received Christ as their Savior. Upon his release, Robbie became a faithful member of Christ Church. Amy's memories of losing her own parents gave her second thoughts about pressing charges. Still, a year passed before she could greet Robbie at the church door on Sundays. It took several more months for her to accept his sixth invitation to sit with him at the fellowship dinner. Three months after that they were engaged. They will be married this summer.

Amy is now the mission board moderator. Some of the women who come to the meetings know Faith through her jail ministry. With their testimonies and the increased attendance, the women's missionary society meetings are far from boring.

Crip

The cool breeze hitting his face was invigorating. The sound of his feet slapping the asphalt and the cheering of the crowd were music to his ears. Kenny loved it. He could never get enough.

Kenny's flowing hair tickled his ears. His mother had chided him about it. She wanted him to get a haircut before the race. But what did she know? Superman had his cape, Kenny had his hair. He felt the sweet little burn in his leg muscles. Nothing to worry about. He glanced over his shoulder. Just one runner within striking distance. Kenny focused on his breathing. Not too hard, nice and steady. With plenty of reserve, he sailed through the backstretch.

Kenny boy, you're the best, he told himself as he pounded home. Nobody in the state, or the world for that matter, can beat you. That trophy is yours. You're the champion. You're headed for the Olympics.

A series of hurdles loomed before him. Kenny's self-aggrandizing pep talk boosted his feeling of power and strength, propelling him over each one without breaking stride. The roar of the crowd pumped his adrenalin. He took his eyes off the yellow tape for a second to glance at his throng of fans. They were on their feet, cheering and whistling, yelling themselves hoarse.

Wanting to give them even more of a thrill, Kenny glanced behind him. Jeremy Hunt, Barnfield High's best runner, was 15 feet behind, his chest heaving like a bellows. Kenny slowed to let Jeremy close the gap. They leveled out. Still, the kid couldn't catch him. Kenny slowed a little more, allowing his rival to think he was tiring. Turning up the heat, Jeremy came alongside.

"Great race, huh, Kenny?" Jeremy grunted, getting no response. Kenny was saving his breath for his last bursting sprint to the finish line.

On both sides of the track, home and visitors, the wooden bleachers thundered with stomping feet and deafening cheers. From the fans' vantage point, the two boys looked to be joined at the hip. Believing Jeremy could pull it out, the Barnfield side went wild. Kenny let out a snort of laughter. Stupid people. Just a few seconds more and he would show them how wrong they were.

Grinning smugly, Kenny's latest girlfriend, Marla, stood with her arms folded over her chest 10 feet from the finish line. She knew what was coming. Kenny had told her enough times. Catching Kenny's eye, Coach Marlow nodded and mouthed "now".

"See ya," Kenny told his rival. Legs pumping, he leaned into the wind. Another hundred meters and victory was his. Pulling easily ahead, Kenny didn't bother to look back. He knew Jeremy was eating his dust. It was the kid's own fault, or maybe his coach's. They both should have known better than to challenge the greatest runner who ever lived.

Kenny ramped it up another notch. The exhilaration of winning shot through him like amphetamine, boosting his speed even further. Jeremy was 20 feet back and fading fast. With a two-lap deficit, the rest of the field limped hopelessly along.

Busting through the tape, Kenny charged across the finish line. With his breathing no more labored than if he'd been walking on the beach, he strolled over to Marla. She handed him a towel and a bottle of water and gave him a peck on the cheek. "My hero. You're the best," she said with a sparkling smile.

"I know," Kenny agreed, grinning.

"You keep running like that and you'll win the gold," Coach Marlow said as he patted his champ on the back.

"Thanks, Coach." Kenny unscrewed the bottle cap and took a swig while watching Jeremy breathlessly cross the finish line. Every visible part of the Barnfield runner's body glistened with sweat. After resting with his hands on his knees for a few moments, he extended his hand to Kenny.

"Great race, bro."

"Yep, it was for me," Kenny snipped, proud of his talent for rudeness. Kenny let the loser stand there holding out his hand while he glanced around. He could see his parents being hustled along by the crowd as they made their way to him. They wouldn't like it if he snubbed the loser. He gave Jeremy's hand a limp shake.

As soon as Jeremy turned to rejoin his team, Marla was at Kenny's side. Standing on tiptoe, she whispered in his ear, "Some guys are duds but you're a stud." She snickered when, making a face, Kenny made a show out of wiping the hand that touched Jeremy's on his shorts.

The expression on Kenny's face said, "So I'm arrogant. Who wouldn't be if they were me?"A thousand times Peter and Dawn Wagner had drummed into their son the importance of being a good sport. But why should he be? He never lost. He'd earned the right to be cock of the walk. When they finally reached him, Kenny noticed his parents' congratulations were a bit restrained.

After the trophy presentation and the usual accolades, there were interviews with the local TV station and newspapers. By the time Kenny made it to the locker room, his teammates had all left. It felt strange being there alone. He felt cheated of the adulation he craved. He had wanted the guys to be there to hoist the greatest runner ever onto their shoulders and shower him with praise. They should have waited. After all, the team, the coach, the school, the fans–everyone owed this win to him.

Things perked up Dom's Pizza. Everybody was there and they all wanted a piece of Kenny. The guys slapped him on the back and clambered to hold the trophy. The girls sidled up to him, lauding him in flirtatious tones while hugging him and kissing his cheeks. When Marla had enough, she led the champ to the last booth in the row, making him slide in first so she could block his admirers from getting to him. But a few persisted, boldly leaning over the back of the bench, tousling his hair and wrapping their arms around his neck.

Kenny didn't seem to mind. His mouth twitched with his effort to stifle a grin as Marla glowered at them. When two of the girls slid into the booth across from them, Marla gave Kenny a dirty look, stood up and headed for the door. "For crying out loud," he muttered, bolting after her. He caught up with her as she bulled her way through a cluster of tables. "Hey, hey, Marla, come on. Don't get mad. It's just a little hero worship. No big deal."

"Of course not. Nothing's a big deal except your ego!" Marla shouted, wrenching her arm from his grip. "I'm leaving." Shoving open the door, she started running across the parking lot, ignoring his pleas as he chased after her. "Come on, Marla, don't be like that."

Reaching Kenny's MG Roadster, Marla turned to confront him. Suddenly her face twisted into a mask of fear. "Kenny, watch out!" she screamed. Kenny saw headlights careening toward him. He felt a terrible pain in his legs. His head bounced off the windshield. For a split second before he slid off the hood, he glimpsed the horrified expressions of the two boys in the front seat. The pain stopped. He felt like he was floating, then nothing.

Two days later, Kenny opened his eyes to sunlight streaming through the window. I'm late for my run was his first thought. During the spring and summer, Kenny would rise at 5:30, sometimes earlier, to run two or three miles in the cool of the predawn mist. It was his favorite thing to do and he rarely missed.

He tried to get up. Where were his legs? He looked down. They were there but he couldn't feel them. No, that's not possible. He tried again. What the–? He looked around. This wasn't his bedroom. Where was he?

Someone entered the room. Kenny turned his head to see Dawn at his bedside, dabbing her eyes with a tissue. She reached down and smoothed his hair. "Welcome back, honey. We almost lost you."

"Mom, what's going on? Where am I?"

"There was an accident."

Kenny's dad appeared, his eyes red-rimmed and swollen, and stood beside Dawn. Avoiding Kenny's questioning eyes, Peter tried to sound upbeat and casual. "We thought you were a goner, sport." His voice broke. Maybe that wasn't the right thing to say.

"Hello, Kenny, how are you feeling?" Dr. Landers said from the open door. What was Kenny's old pediatrician doing here?

"I can't feel my legs," Kenny whimpered. His voice shook with fear; a tremor of panic surged through him. He wanted to know why, yet was terrified of the answer.

The doctor sat on the edge of the bed. Except for his white hair, he hadn't changed since he removed Kenny's tonsils when Kenny was nine. Landers had seen the young boy's fear and explained the simple operation to him to assure him all would be well. As he was wheeled into surgery, Kenny gripped his mother's hand as she walked alongside. She was allowed to stay in the operating room until the anesthesia took effect. Later, over a bowl of ice cream, Kenny laughed about his fear.

Now the elderly doctor removed his glasses and set them on the bedside table. He laid his hand on Kenny's arm. "Kenny, the accident damaged some nerves in your spine, which caused paralysis in your legs. I'm afraid the prognosis isn't encouraging."

"What are you saying?" Kenny asked, fighting back tears.

Dr. Landers sighed. "Son, I'm afraid you may never walk again. And even if by some miracle you do, your days as a track star are over."

Kenny shook his head slowly on the pillow. Disbelief and denial quickly took control. "No, no, I'm going to the Olympics. I'm the best runner there ever was. Oh, no, NO! This can't be happening!" he screamed, shaking off the doctor's hand. He hammered his fists on the bed. He's wrong! He has to be wrong!

Squeezing shut his eyes, Kenny rubbed his tears away with the heels of his hands. He didn't want them to see him bawling. He was tough. He was the star of his team. No one was stronger. He turned his face away, pressing it into the pillow. "Leave me alone," he blubbered through muffled sobs. Doctor Landers stood up and stepped to the foot of the bed.

Awkwardly, Dawn tried to hug him, her arms curling around the wires and tubes. He shrugged her off. He looked up at their pitying faces and went livid. "I said leave me alone!" Kenny shouted, beating the mattress with his fists. His face twisted into an ugly mask. The veins in his neck bulged and throbbed. "Get out of here! Get OUT!"

"Come on folks," Dr. Landers said softly, gently ushering Peter and Dawn toward the door. "Why don't you go get something to eat? Kenny and I need to have a little talk." Closing the door behind the bewildered man and sobbing woman, Landers pushed a chair next to the bed and sat quietly. Kenny tried to ignore him.

"Kenny, I've known you since you were just a few days old. You were always the child with the sunniest disposition. I looked forward to your coming in for your check-ups because you never failed to brighten my day, even the difficult ones. But you've changed. True, I haven't seen you much since you've grown up. But enough to know. And people talk. They say you've become arrogant and conceited, so much so that they really don't want to be around you. You've developed a superior attitude and–"

"I'm better than them! I'm the fastest runner in the history of the school. I'm the most important person on the team." Tears of anger and frustration streamed down Kenny's face.

"Let's say you are. What about the people who helped you? Who encouraged you? Your mother and father. They played a part in your success. Your coaches. Do you think you'd be where you are today without them?"

"You mean where I *was*. Not anymore. I'm lying in a hospital bed with my legs crushed. Just say it! I'm a lousy cripple. A stinking crip."

"If that's your attitude, Kenny, then you're right. You'll never walk again. Listen to me, my boy. There are thousands, millions of physically healthy people in this world who are cripples, not in their bodies but in their minds. Don't be one of them." Without another word, Dr. Landers got up and left the room.

"Who does he think he is, telling me how to live?" Kenny turned his face to the wall and wept. When the tears finally stopped, he stared up at the ceiling, unable to purge Landers' words from his thoughts. Arrogant, conceited, superior. That hurt. He took a long, hard look at his life. What did he have to show for it? A few trophies? Friends who were friends only if he kept winning? A girlfriend who disappeared the moment he was no longer Super Jock?

What kind of life was that?

The realization that he would never be the same made Kenny's blood run cold. If the doctor was right, he'd never walk again. Someone would have to wheel him wherever he needed to go. No more would he revel in the power of his feet pounding the track or the exhilaration of the cool breeze rushing over his body. No more would a thrill surge through him when he broke the tape at the finish line. His classmates' adoration, gone. The cute, giggling girls, gone.

As for Marla, Kenny had always known she only hung around with him because he was the track star. She didn't care about him, only what he could do for her. He looked good on her arm. Truth be told, he dated her for the same reason. All the guys wanted Marla. She was a head-turning beauty, the prettiest girl in school. But Kenny found the other side of Marla–her mean-spiritedness, vainness, self-absorption and shallowness–hard to take. Even if he hadn't become a crip, it wouldn't have been long before they parted ways. So now his crumpled legs would take care of the break-up for him.

But after analyzing Marla and the others, Kenny had to admit that he was no different. Dr. Landers was right; Kenny was selfish, caring nothing for others, only himself. Reliving his cockiness on and off the track, he winced with shame. You need to change, my man, he told himself. He knew what it would take. For the first time in over a year, Kenny prayed, asking the Lord to bless and use him in any way He wanted.

When Peter and Dawn returned, it was clear their son had undergone a transformation. Kenny was his old self–the bright-eyed, cheerful, humble son they had known before fame and pride spoiled him. Kenny's parents looked at each other first with surprise, then delight. Over the next few weeks, Kenny's winning smile and upbeat attitude brightened the day of all those around him. His optimism was a breath of fresh air to the hospital staff and other patients with whom he came into contact.

Every morning after breakfast and before therapy, Kenny rolled his wheelchair into the children's ward. He made funny faces to get them to laugh and forget their pain and confinement. He comforted the hurting and encouraged the down-hearted.

Kenny's rehabilitation proceeded slowly. At first, he couldn't move his legs without clasping his hands around them to lift them up. He sat on the edge of his bed lifting and releasing them for an hour each day. With no response, he had to fight off his fear that the exercise was futile.

Late at night, dark thoughts flooded his mind. He dreamed of being in a race, looking over his shoulder at his competitors and laughing at their feeble efforts. In the next instant, he was lying on the ground and watching them thunder past him to the finish line. Quietly, he wet his pillow with his tears.

Two months after the accident, Kenny was using his hands one morning to swing his leg. His toe hit the bed rail. "Ouch, that hur…" He suddenly realized he could feel the bedding under the soles of his feet. He swung his foot hard against the rail again, just to be sure. The pain traveled from his foot to his calf to his thigh.

When Dawn came in at nine, she found Kenny standing unassisted next to the bed. A nurse was stationed by his side to catch him if he teetered. Gathering Kenny in her arms, his mother began to weep. She told him of her prayers for his recovery, spiritual and physical.

The next week was a whirlwind of activity, ending with him leaving the hospital on Friday. As the nurse wheeled him out of his room, Kenny couldn't believe his eyes. Lining both sides of the hallway were the children from pediatrics and the staff. Doctor Landers stepped forward and shook Kenny's hand. "I'm proud of you, son," he said, smiling. Someone started clapping. Soon the hallway was ringing with cheers and applause. The kids raised their fists in victory. Their applause meant more to Kenny than winning the gold at the Olympics.

Over his objections, Kenny's parents made the den into a bedroom. "It's just until you can navigate the stairs," Peter told his son. A few of Kenny's friends from school came by, their faces registering disappointment when he told them his days on the track were finished. Marla was not among the visitors. He saw on her Facebook page that she had attached herself to the football team's quarterback. Kenny couldn't help feeling sorry for the guy.

On Saturday afternoon, Jeremy Hunt rang the doorbell. Answering the door, Dawn smiled at the nervous boy. "I remember you. You competed with Kenny in his last race."

"Yes, ma'am. He was really fast." Jeremy didn't know what else to say.

"I'm glad you came. Kenny gets so lonely," Dawn said as she ushered Jeremy into the den. "Kenny, look who came to visit." Jeremy stepped tentatively into the room, unsure if he would be welcome.

Dawn left them alone. Sitting on the edge of his bed, Kenny remembered his attitude the last time he saw

Jeremy. He wanted to apologize but wasn't sure how. The two boys stared at each other."I... I've been praying for you since the accident," Jeremy finally said. "I was going to come see you in the hospital but thought I should wait–"

"That's okay," Kenny interrupted, trying to get past the awkwardness.

"You were always a better runner then me," Jeremy said.

"No, I'm not." Kenny said, smiling at his former rival.

"Yeah you were, Kenny. Every time we ran against each other, you won."

"Jeremy, the reason I won is because I knew how to control my breathing," Kenny said, realizing he actually liked this kid. "Your pacing is great, but you use up all your breath during the race. By the end you're all out and you have to drag in more air to finish."

"Wow. So that's the secret to winning?"

"There are other factors, but breathing is an important one."

"Can you show me how to breathe that way?"

"Sure." Kenny was genuinely glad to do it. For the next half hour, he taught Jeremy how to breathe correctly and explained some the other techniques Coach Marlow had taught him.

After promising to let Kenny know the result of his next race, Jeremy left, ecstatic. The following Saturday he was back. His face shone with excitement as he told Kenny how he had trained all week, practicing the breathing method he taught him. "The race against Parkview yesterday? Believe it or not, I won. I wasn't even out of breath when I crossed the finish line. I owe it all to you, brother."

Kenny smiled broadly. "What do you mean, believe it or not? All I did was show you how to control your breathing. You did it yourself. You know why? Because you're a winner. You just needed somebody to convince you of it."

Listening in the next room, Dawn smiled. Tears misted her eyes. She had never been prouder of her son.

Millie's Promise

George McMillan entered the break room just as Millie was finishing her coffee. "I'm gonna to need you to work Saturday," he informed her. "Kelsey's going to her cousin's wedding, so I'm short a cashier."

That was a lie. It was common knowledge among the SuperMart employees that George and Kelsey were having an affair. Being the only one in the break room and having the most to lose if she balked, Millie was McMillan's choice as the one to take Kelsey's shift.

With her shoes off and her feet propped on a chair, Millie had been relishing her 15 minutes of peace and quiet before having to get back to the grind. At the sight of George, she dropped her feet and shoved them into her well-worn sneakers. Wearing those shoes was the only way Millie could stand at the checkout for eight hours. Allowing her to wear them was the one concession George had made to anyone asking to deviate from the standard uniform. There were many issues between SuperMart's management and staff, not the least of which was the fact that the company made the women purchase their own uniforms while providing them to the male employees for free.

Averting her eyes, Millie said, "I can't, Mr. McMillan. I promised Bobby I'd take him camping this weekend." Millie's heart pounded as fear and contempt bubbled up

within. Over the past several months, she had covered for
Kelsey at least a dozen times, knowing full well it was only
so her coworker could sneak off to some motel with
McMillan. Their tryst and her connection to it, albeit
indirect, disgusted Millie, but she desperately needed this
job. This week's pay would make only a small dent in the
bills that were piling up. If she got fired, she and Bobby
would be on the street within a month.

At this time last year, Millie was happily married, or at
least she thought so. While sorting her husband's clothes
for the wash one morning, she found a note in his pants
pocket. The message from the blond bombshell at Charles's
office was a graphic recount of what the two of them had
done the last time they shared a motel room. The laundry
forgotten, Millie dissolved in tears. Thank God their 10-
year-old son, Bobby, was in school. Millie's emotions
swirled from shock to rage to revenge and back again as
she paced the house like a nervous cat. Three times she
almost called the office. She got only as far as punching in
the number before thinking better of it and hitting the end
button.

Late that afternoon, Millie sent Bobby to his friend's house
for a play date. When Charles came through the front door,
he was met by a confused and angry wife. Millie held out
the note like a shield. "Well, I'm glad it's over," Charles
said. An odd smile somewhere between shame and relief
crossed his face. Assuming he was referring to the affair,
Millie was unprepared for his next words: "Guess I better
pack my bags and be gone before Bobby gets home." They
pierced Millie's heart like a spear.

"Speaking of our son, what do you suggest I tell him? That
his father left us for a slut?

Charles stiffened. "Sorry to break it to you, Millie, but she's no slut. She's a very respectable woman. She's gentle and kind and she takes care of herself." He left off "unlike you," but the inference was there.

"Oh, yes, what she's been doing with a married man is highly respectable. So what happens when you get tired of her? Do you trade her in for a new model? Or are you just going to cheat on her until she finds out, like I did?"

"I don't have time for this." Heaving a huge sigh and swearing under his breath, Charles made his way up the stairs to their bedroom. He was back in minutes with a suitcase in his hand and two suits slung over his shoulder. There's no way he could pack that fast, Millie thought. She remembered seeing the bag in the back of the closet but, being the last one to know, never thought to open it. Now it was clear that Charles had been preparing for his exit while waiting for the other shoe to drop.

Before Millie could speak he was out the door, slamming it behind him. She watched through the living room window as his car roared out of the driveway and disappeared down the street. The pain in her heart was crushing. She collapsed on the sofa and wept.

When Bobby came home, Millie lied that his dad had gone on a business trip. Holding herself together until Bobby was tucked into bed, she retreated to her room. Overcome with shock, loss and grief, all she could do was crawl into bed, bury her face in the pillow and let it pour out.

Two days later, a courier stood at the front door holding divorce papers. Dazed, Millie sat at the computer and half-heartedly began searching for a job. When Bobby came home from school, she sat him down and, as gently as she could, told him his father would not be living with them anymore. Pulling the weeping child into her arms, Millie wept with him.

Over the next few weeks, aside from a few crying spells, Bobby seemed to adjust to his father's absence. In truth, Charles had never been much of a factor in Bobby's life. Still, it was clear from the far-away look in his eyes that the boy missed him terribly. Millie did her best to fill the gap, although her state of confusion, loss and uncertainty robbed her of energy and enthusiasm.

On one of his infrequent visits, Charles promised to take Bobby camping the following weekend. When Friday night rolled around, Bobby was so wound up he barely slept. At ten to six Saturday morning, Millie heard him rummaging around in the kitchen. Yawning, she descended the stairs to find him checking and repacking his duffle bag as he had at least a half dozen times during the week.

Wanting to sleep in on her day off, Millie nevertheless stayed up and made breakfast. Afraid he would miss his father, Bobby kept going to the window. At 7:30, he took up a position on the sidewalk. Millie kept her eye on him as she cleaned up the kitchen. An hour passed. Heartbroken, Millie watched her son pull his spyglass from his pack and used it to look up and down the street. She called Charles's cell and left a voice mail message. "Your son is waiting on the curb for you." Afraid she would say something she'd regret later, she bit her tongue and ended the call.

At nine, Millie went outside and tried to persuade Bobby to come in the house. With angry tears streaming, he refused. In her heart, Millie felt the same pain she had the day she found out about Charles's infidelity. After waiting another hour, Bobby was forced to face the cold, hard fact that he could not rely on his father. Shrugging Millie's hand off his shoulder, the boy stomped into the garage, hurled his pack into the corner and ran upstairs to his bedroom. From the hallway outside his locked door, Millie heard him sobbing.

By noon Millie had called Charles's phone three more times. All went to voice mail. The house was too quiet and Millie began to worry about Bobby being behind that locked door. At one o'clock, she stood in front of it with a ham sandwich and a glass of milk. "Bobby, honey, please open the door. I brought you some lunch."

She heard him cross the room and pull back the latch. "Why Mom, why does Dad hate me?" Bobby asked as she entered. Millie was at a loss, her heart breaking again. How do you explain to a child that his father chose an adulterous affair over his family? With no words to comfort him, she gathered her sobbing son in her arms and held him until he fell asleep.

She just stepped into the kitchen when her cell phone rang. Glancing at the screen, she saw Charles's number. Seething with rage, she thought of not answering, but for Bobby's sake she punched the button.

"Yes?" she snapped, clipping off the word.

"Hi Millie." Charles sounded strange, his voice high-pitched and stressed.

"Hi Millie nothin'. Where were you?" Her heart raced, her face flamed and she was finding it hard to breath. Calm down, she told herself. "Your son waited at the curb for you all morning."

"I... forgot," he said, so quietly she could barely hear. Charles always mumbled when was lying.

Steaming, Millie's knuckles turned white as she squeezed the phone as hard as she wanted to squeeze his neck. "You forgot. How noble of you. I'm sure Bobby would be so proud of his father to hear that."

"Okay, okay. Lighten up, will you?" Charles sounded to Millie like a whining adolescent. "Would you please just tell him something came up at the office and I'll make it up to him soon?"

"Hey c'mon, babe, we're going to be late," a female voice in the background called.

"Say hi to the slut for me," Millie said bitterly.

"Yeah, well, you'll be happy to know that didn't work out. Listen, Millie, I really am sorry. I'll make it up to Bobby. I promise."

"You and your promises. But it's nice that you at least remembered his name." There was silence. "You're pathetic," Millie said, her voice dripping with hatred and disgust.

"I don't want to fight, Mill. Tell Bobby I'll call him later." The phone went dead.

Breathing hard, Millie reared back her arm with the impulse to smash the phone against the fireplace. Instead, she laid it on the coffee table and went upstairs to check on her son.

As it turned out, that was the first of Charles's many broken promises. After the third, Bobby didn't bother to pack his camping equipment. Nor did he show any emotion when Charles didn't show. He simply went to his room without a word and stayed there all day. As fall turned to winter, the promise of a camping trip was swept away with the wind.

From then on, anytime Millie saw Charles's name on the caller ID, she would let it ring. He never left a message. Millie wasn't surprised when Charles left Bobby's Christmas present on the doorstep with a note that he would call later. But it still hurt. She spent the day stewing in her loneliness while Bobby went sledding with his friends.

At the beginning of May, Millie surprised Bobby with plans for a camping trip. Hardly a nature girl, she nevertheless would endure any discomfort for her son. Unenthused at first, Bobby grew more excited as the time approached. Unlike his father, Millie had never made Bobby a promise she didn't keep.

Charles sent money whenever he felt like it, and that wasn't often. Lacking skills, Millie had searched for weeks before finally landing the cashier's job at SuperMart. She soon learned that George McMillan was a hard taskmaster unless you were one of his favorites. He was known to find a reason to fire anyone who questioned his management policies. Then there was the ongoing rumor that George was stepping out on his wife. It was a standing joke in the break room. Just for giggles, some of the female employees would tease him just enough to let him think he had a chance. Kelsey, on the other hand, wasn't fooling. She had her hooks into old George and led him around by the proverbial ring in his nose.

Now as McMillan stood over her breathing fire, Millie's skin crawled. Never before had she refused to comply. An attractive woman at 35, she drew the line at McMillan's advances, but always in a restrained and polite manner. Now, even as her heart pounded in her chest, she wasn't going to be sweet. She needed this job. She was three months behind in the mortgage, the tires on the car were bald and the electric company was threatening to shut her off. Regardless, she would not let Bobby down.

"I can't do it this weekend, Mr. McMillan," she repeated. "I made a promise to Bobby."

"Just tell him you gotta work. He'll get over it."

"I'm sorry, but no." Millie wondered if she looked as nervous as she felt, but her resolve didn't waver.

McMillan twisted his face into a thuggish snarl and leaned so close to Millie she flinched. "If you're not here at eight in the morning don't brother coming back Monday."

Tears formed in the corners of Millie's eyes. "Please, Mr. McMillan. I need this job."

"Then you'll be here tomorrow morning. Not traipsing around the woods with your kid."

"I can't!" Millie shrieked, nearly making herself jump. Tears streamed down her crimson cheeks. Dropping her head, she tried to compose herself. "I can work next Saturday or 'til closing on Monday," she murmured.

"Forget it. You're fired. Leave the uniform in the locker."

"What? But I bought this uniform."

"Leave it or I'll charge you with theft." George gave her a smarmy grin.

"I have the receipt."

McMillan was beginning to enjoy this. He'd never pegged little Millie for having such guts. He leered at her. "Take it off or I'll take it off you."

"You know what? Try. I'll report you to the district office."

McMillan skewed his lips into a repugnant sneer. "And I'll have you arrested for stealing from the till. You think I can't? Ask around and see how many times I've done it. Who's gonna take care of your kid while you're in the slammer? He'll end up in foster care."

"You're ridiculous. Uh, can you say evidence?" Millie taunted, growing bolder with his every threat.

"Manager's word against a lowly little dumb cashier's? Evidence enough. Now take that thing off or I'll rip it off." He grabbed at the buttons on her bodice.

Backing away, Millie slapped his hand.

"Touch me and I'll scream so loud they'll hear me in the parking lot!" she shouted.

George dropped his hand and stood staring at her until she blinked. "You ain't got nothin' worth seeing anyway." He leaned over her again. "I want you outta here in five minutes. And you better leave that dress or I'm calling the cops." He whirled on his heel and was gone.

Flabbergasted and scared silly, Millie stared after him. She had just lost her only source of income. Charles was six months behind in child support. Millie knew taking him to court would do no good. When finalizing the divorce, the judge set the child support award for two years and told her not to ask for an increase any sooner.

With little left to lose other than her cheesy uniform, Millie cracked open the break room door and saw George at the front of the store. Taking a deep breath, she ran through the storeroom and burst through the rear door. The shrieking alarm overhead pierced her ears like a jackhammer. Running like a thief across the weed-strewn back lot, she made it to her car, fumbled with the lock, jumped in and jammed the key in the ignition. Unnerved, she floored the accelerator and let out a yelp when the car lurched forward.

Whining in protest, the engine stalled. Tears blurred Millie's vision as she turned the key. "Oh, please, not now." The world was crashing down on her. Never in her life had she felt such fear.

The motor caught just as George pushed open the back door. Spotting her, he raised his fist and shouted, "I'm callin' the cops!" Shifting into gear, Millie roared past him. Stopping at the entrance to the street, she looked in the rearview mirror. Even at this distance his beady, glowering eyes bored through her. She half expected him to come charging after her. Instead, he stepped back and pulled shut the door.

The police car pulled up behind her at the light on Jefferson. When it turned green, he turned on his light bar. Millie pulled to the side with her heart in her throat. The cop did a U-turn and turned on his siren. Millie gripped the wheel with her trembling hands and waited for her stomach to stop heaving, then drove the few blocks home. Thankful that Bobby was still in school, she turned the key in the front door and stepped into the foyer.

The house was deathly silent, gloomy as a tomb. Bobby's camping pack lay by the back door, looking so forlorn it brought tears to Millie's eyes. Burying her face in her hands, she cried. Her crying became sobs, her sobs turned to wails. How much more could she take? Another month and the bank would foreclose on the house. The car was falling apart. The electric bill with its accumulated late charges had chewed up most of her last paycheck. There was less than $20 in her checking account.

Swallowing her pride, Millie called Charles. In a voice as shrill as a fishwife's, she recorded her message. "Charles, I'm out of money. If you don't send at least a thousand immediately I'm taking you to court." Ending the call she sat shaking her head. It was an empty threat, and Charles would know it. The law would do nothing. Even if they locked him up for nonsupport, he would just get further behind.

Over the next hour, Millie vacillated between hope and despair. She had to keep her promise. The only way she wouldn't was if the cops hauled her off on George's theft charge. She counted her cash. Just $50. The campground fee for two nights was 15, gas for the car 10. That left 25 for food and incidentals. The cloud seemed to lift. She would deal with everything Monday morning. This weekend she would focus on giving Bobby the best camping trip ever, one he'd remember for the rest of his life.

It was almost noon. Bobby would be at lunch. If they left now they could be at the campground by one. Millie packed up the car and headed to the school. Bobby had just sat down across the table from his best friend, Justin, when he heard his name over the PA system. "Bobby Freeman, please report to the principal's office.

"Uh oh, boy, you're in trouble now," Justin teased.

Bobby marched down the hall on wooden legs. Nobody went to the principal's office unless they were in big trouble. Timidly, he knocked on the door. It opened and his mother stepped out, holding her finger to her lips. Looking back into the office, she said, "Thank you. I think we'll just make his appointment." Laying a hand Bobby's shoulder, she propelled him down the hallway.

"What appointment, Mom?" Bobby asked as they walked to the car.

"Our appointment to go camping," Millie answered with a sly grin.

"For real?" Opening the car door, Bobby spotted the camping equipment in the back seat. His face brightened, then fell. "What about the doctor's note? They'll ask me for one on Monday."

"Let me worry about that. What do you say we start this adventure with some ice cream?" Before Charles's departure, the family would visit the Dairy Queen at least once a week. This would be the first time in months that Millie and Bobby treated themselves to anything. Millie's heart almost broke when he offered to help pay for his cone. He pulled the few coins from his pocket and held them out to her.

"No, honey, that's all right," she said, mentally calculating the bills in her purse. "This is my treat." The car payment was due Tuesday. Millie would worry about it then. Bobby deserved this camping trip, and he was going to have it.

The ride to the campground was relaxing, the weather perfect. After finishing their cones, mother and son held a songfest, seeing who could sing the loudest. Bobby won hands down. Then he dozed off. Driving through the countryside, worry nagged at Millie. Would McMillan really stoop so low as to have her arrested? Could she get out of it just by showing the cops the receipt? If not and she landed in jail, Bobby would have to live with Charles, the father who cared more about the women he cheated with than he did his own son. Millie pushed the unpleasant thoughts to the back of her mind. At the campground gate, she peeled a 10 and a five off her dwindling roll of bills.

The camping area consisted of a clearing large enough to accommodate 25 sites. Only three were occupied. They picked out a spot on the south side and started unloading the car.

Putting the rest of the camping gear aside, Millie took out the instructions for setting up the tent. They seemed straightforward enough. After spreading out the tent, she placed the poles around its edges. The instructions advised that pitching the tent was a two-man job. Millie snickered when she read that. How difficult can it be? She tussled with it for 20 minutes, with Bobby doing his best to help. Just when she thought she had it, after struggling her way into its center the poles toppled and the tent collapsed on her.

"Would you like me to help?"

The voice sounded close. I must look like a blithering idiot, Millie thought. Flailing her way out from under the billowing canvas, she blinked at the handsome stranger. Mortified, she sloughed the thing off her back and let it fall to the ground.

"Not as easy as I thought," she murmured, lowering her head to hide her flushed face from the staring, smiling man. He was slim, muscular and at least 6'2" with dark brown hair and twinkling brown eyes. She guessed him to be in his late 30's.

He stooped to pick up one of the poles."I can put it up for you. They do tend to be a bit tricky."

Millie blew a wisp of hair out of her eyes. "That would be greatly appreciated. We'll help."

"My dad usually does it but he's not here," Bobby said sadly.

"Let me see what I can do." The stranger picked up a second pole and fitted the two together. Millie watched in wonder as he singlehandedly erected the tent in a matter of minutes.

"There," he said, "that should do it."

"Thank you so much, Mr. ..."

"Eric. Eric Hicks. And you are?"

"Millie Freeman. And this is my son, Bobby." Eric shook Millie's hand, then Bobby's. Millie noticed his handshake was firm, yet gentle.

"Hey, Bobby, I have a boy around here somewhere," Eric said. Scanning the campground, he called, "Benny, Ben! Come meet these folks."

A boy about the same age as Bobby emerged from the forest. "Hey, Dad, there's a chipmunk over there living in a hollow log," Ben said, pointing to the way he came. He looked at Bobby. "Wanna go see it?"

"Can I, Mom?" Bobby said, turning with pleading eyes to his mother.

"Okay. But don't go too far. And be careful!" The words barely left Millie's mouth before the boys were off and running.

"Don't worry," Eric told her."Ben knows these woods. Sometimes I think he spends more time here than at home."

"Do you live close by, Mr. Hicks?"

"Eric, please. Yes. Just across the highway a little north of here."

"That must be lovely. The only park we have in the city is a small one ten blocks from our home."

"Yes, it is nice to have this practically in our back yard. Unfortunately, my work keeps me away more than I'd like.

Well, Millie–may I call you Millie? If you need anything
I'm right over there." He pointed to a campsite about 50
feet away.

"Thanks again, Mr.–"

"Eric," he corrected with a broad smile.

"Eric. Thank you again for putting up the tent," Millie said,
smiling shyly back at him.

Millie couldn't help but steal a few glances at him while
she set up camp. He was good-looking in a rugged kind of
way. She tried to guess what type of job he had. With those
muscles, he must do a lot of lifting. Warehouse?
Construction? Eric was built for heavy lifting, all right, but
not the kind Millie was thinking. Catching her looking at
him, he smiled and waved. Self-consciously, Millie waved
back, then ducked under the car's open trunk lid, her
cheeks red with embarrassment.

Having lain everything out on the ground, Millie looked for
the camp stove. It had to be here. All the food she brought
had to be heated. How could she have forgotten the camp
stove? Depressed, she sat down on a log and hung her head.
Why was all this happening to her? Everything was
supposed to be perfect for Bobby. How could she hand him
a can of cold beans? She rummaged through the picnic
basket. She wanted to cry. No can opener, no spoons, no
knife. Here she got herself fired just to do a good thing for
Bobby, and instead they were in the middle of nowhere
with nothing to eat. If it hadn't been for Eric, they'd be
sleeping in the car. She wanted to kick herself.

Bobby was back, breathing hard from running. Millie had
packed several cans of soda, but in her haste and with little
money the thought of buying ice escaped her. Grabbing a
root beer, Bobby called, "Hey, Mom, these are warm!

Where's the ice?"

"We're roughing it, remember?" Millie said, forcing a smile.

Shaking his head, Bobby took a swig and grimaced as he swallowed it down. "Benny and me are going fishing after supper. If that's okay."

"We'll see. Maybe Benny's father and I will come along."

The aroma of grilled meat permeated the campground. "Boy, that smells good," Bobby said. "When are we going to fire up our grill? I'll help."

Frustrated and ashamed to admit her negligence, Millie avoided her son's questioning look. "I think we'll wait awhile."

"Dad wants to know if you wanna come eat with us," Benny hollered as he ran toward them. Catching his breath when he reached them, he added, "We have plenty of steaks. Dad works at a grocery store and gets stuff for cheap."

Seated at the edge of the campfire with a plate loaded with grilled potatoes, corn on the cob and the biggest steak she ever saw, Millie said, "This is great, Eric. You're a really good cook."

"Thank you."

"Mom works at a grocery store too," Bobby piped up. "Ever heard of SuperMart?"

Ben opened his mouth. "Anybody up for another steak?" Eric asked loudly, shooting a look at his son to keep quiet."I can stoke up these coals if you're still hungry." There were no takers.

"Thanks," Millie said. "It was great but I couldn't eat another bite."

Clean-up done, Millie and Eric sat on a log watching the boys play catch. Her mind wouldn't stop nagging her. Ask him. Looking straight ahead, she forced out the words. "Any possibility your store is hiring?"

Eric thought for a moment. "You know, I think I did hear the boss say we could use another person. Mind if I ask what happened with your last job?"

Millie was reluctant to tell him, but once she started talking the story tumbled out. When she finished, she was embarrassed at how foolish she must look. "I'm sorry... I didn't... I mean... sorry."

"Don't be. This George character sounds like a real jerk."

Millie nodded. "Until the district manager comes around. Then he's all sweetness and light."

"Let's see if the boys still want to go fishing. And listen, don't worry, okay? I think I can get my boss to bring you on board."

The camping trip turned out to be more fun than Millie imagined it could be. Eric insisted that she and Bobby join Ben and him for every meal. Although a bit tight-lipped about his life, Eric was a great conversationalist. Millie found him captivating and was very comfortable talking with him. He also was a good listener, a trait she'd seen in very few men.

On Sunday morning, they packed up early and returned home to attend services at their respective churches.

Monday morning after sending Bobby off to school, Millie

sat at the kitchen table going through the bills. She grew more tense and frightened as the words "due" and "past-due" jumped up at her from each one. Even if–and that was a big IF–Charles came up with the thousand, it wouldn't be enough. The delinquent house payments would eat up most of it. Then there was the car. She needed two, possibly three thousand just to get her head above water. She could think of only one solution. Grabbing the phone book, Millie opened it to "Realtors".

She didn't want to give up her home. She fell in love with it the first time she saw it. Bobby was only a few weeks old when they moved in. Millie spent weeks cleaning, painting and making it their own. She planted flowerbeds in front of the house and around the property's perimeter, tending them lovingly throughout the spring and summer.

Pushing through her sadness, Millie selected an agent and picked up the phone. Just as she did, it rang. She didn't recognize the number. Then she remembered Eric slipping her a piece of paper with his number. She dug it out of her purse and saw it was the same. Maybe he talked to his boss. Punching in the number, she waited nervously.

"Hi, Millie!" Eric said. Hearing his voice made Millie smile. "Hey, if you're still interested, I may have a job for you."

"Oh, I'm definitely interested. So, you spoke to your supervisor?"

"Yes. He thinks you'd be perfect for this job. Can you come down to SuperMart right away?"

"SuperMart!" Millie started tearing up. "No, Eric. I don't think I can."

"Trust me, Millie. Meet me at the Burger King across from

the store."

"I…" He hung up before she could refuse. Could she trust him? She barely knew him. She looked down at the Realtor's ad She would take the risk and trust him. Grabbing her purse, Millie drove the few blocks to the restaurant, wracking her brain along the way. How could Eric work at SuperMart? She knew all the employees there and she sure wouldn't have missed him.

No sooner had she parked the car than Eric was standing at the driver's side window. He wore a French cut suit, a red and white striped tie and a serious expression. Two men also wearing suits stood behind him. "Leave the car here," Eric told her. "It'll be all right. I've already spoken to the manager."

He took off at a fast pace with the two men in tow. Lagging behind, Millie said loudly, "Wait, wait! You talked to the manager?"

Not breaking stride, Eric turned and walked backward as he answered, "Of the Burger King. So your car doesn't get towed." He whirled around, crossed the street and stopped to the left of the SuperMart entrance where he couldn't be seen from inside. Breathing heavily, Millie caught up with them.

"Millie, I need you to do me a big favor. I want you to go in and ask George for your paycheck."

Millie looked at him quizzically. Who exactly are you? she wondered. But he was waiting for her response. "Eric, I can't do that. When he fired me, he said if I came back here he would have me arrested for stealing."

One of the men piped up. "I wouldn't worry about that, Miss. There will be an arrest here today, but it won't be you."

"I'm sorry, Millie," Eric said."I was so focused on bringing McMillan down I forgot to introduce these gentlemen to you. Indicating the man in the gray suit, he introduced Detective Roy Moore. "And this is Ralph Boxsy, my district manager. You've probably seen him before."

"See that van over there with the tinted windows?" Moore asked her, nodding toward a white Econoline parked in the corner of the lot. "It's wired. With Mr. Hicks' permission, we bugged McMillan's office last night."

Millie looked at Eric. "*Your* district manager? You're not just an employee at SuperMart, are you?"

"No. I own this chain and a few other companies. Millie, McMillan has been embezzling for years. We estimate he's taken over a million dollars."

"We have some evidence, Millie. But if you can get him to admit he's been stealing, we'll have an airtight case against him," Moore added.

Looking from one man to the next, Millie nodded. "Let's do this."

Moore spoke into his radio. "Stand by."

McMillan was in his office with the door just enough ajar for Millie to glimpse him leaning over his desk as she approached. She pushed open the door and strode in. "I came for my check, George," she said firmly.

He straightened up and gave her a leering once-over. "You got some nerve, girlie. Your crummy little check won't even cover the cost of that dress you stole. I'll have to make up the difference out of my pocket. Now get out of here."

Taking a step forward, Millie closed the door and leaned against it. She knew her face was flushed; she could feel it burning. She prayed George couldn't hear her heart pounding. They're right outside listening, she told herself. She tried to swallow the baseball-sized lump in her throat. "I know what you've been doing." Barely hearing the words herself, she cleared her throat and repeated them.

George leaned on the edge of the desk and crossed his arms. "Sweetheart, you got more guts than brains. Okay, what have I been doing?" He raised his eyebrows and stuck out his chin as if to say, come on, make it good.

"I know why the cash in the registers always comes up short." Millie reached around and gripped the doorknob.

He took a step toward her.

"Really? And why is that, Princess?"

"Very simple, George. The cars you drive, the house you live in, the vacations you take. I think the police will be very interested in having a look at your bank statements."

McMillan came at her, stopping just inches from her nose. Millie locked her knees and held onto the doorknob as the room swirled around her. She was sure she was going to faint.

"Now you listen to me. If you try that, you know what will happen? Nothing." McMillan laughed in her face, nearly knocking her off her feet. "Not to me anyway. I'll keep on stealing from these jerks like I have for the last ten years. And if they ever figure it out, which they won't, you can read all about it in your prison cell."

Millie turned the doorknob slowly. "They'll believe me."

"Yeah, sure they will after I plant a few marked bills in places you wouldn't think to look. Oh, and I have a witness." He picked up the phone. "Send Kelsey in here."

"So Kelsey's in on it. Big surprise."

George laughed. "Oh, honey, with that moron running the head office I don't need any help. Wanna know what my take has been so far?"

"A hundred thousand?" Millie's dumb act worked splendidly. The blowhard braggadocio couldn't resist impressing the poor little loser with the enormity of his exploits.

Backing up, George sat on the edge of his desk, smiling and dangling his leg. He waited a few seconds, just to pump up the suspense. "Try two point three mil and change." He threw back his head and howled with laughter. "Two million—"

Millie leapt aside as the door was thrown open. Moore stormed in, followed by Boxsy and several uniformed police officers."George McMillan, you're under arrest for embezzlement."

Stunned, McMillan's face drained of color as he pointed at Millie. "Wait a minute," he sputtered. "She's the thief! I caught her stealing from the register." The officers spun him around and cuffed him. "Mr. Boxsy, Mr. Boxsy. C'mon. You know I'd never steal from you."

"Nice try, Georgie boy," Ralph Boxsy taunted as the blubbering crook was hustled out of the office. George caught sight of Eric standing just outside the doorway. Taking a recorder from his pocket, Eric flipped it on and played back George's words as the officers frog-marched their suspect down the hall. Watching them pass through the aisles and out the door, the SuperMart employees cheered and applauded.

Stepping back into the office, Eric smiled at a pale-faced Millie leaning limply against the wall. "We did it," he said. "You did it. You were great, Millie." Eric took her hand and led her to a chair.

"I'm just glad it's over," Millie said in a near whisper.

"Well, now I need a manager. A trustworthy one. What do you say? Want the job?"

"Me?" Millie asked incredulously.

"I can't think of anyone more qualified. By the way, the job comes with a five thousand dollar signing bonus. Interested?"

And that's how Millie Freeman became manager of SuperMart. The position, however, was temporary. She soon went on to bigger and better things. Having chosen a lifelong career as Mrs. Eric Hicks, Millie has found fulfillment as wife, homemaker and full-time mom to Bobby and Ben.

The Road to Nowhere

Nowhere started out as a pockmark in a dirt road winding through the plains of west Texas. Far from everything, near to nothing, it was named as a joke by some ranchers passing through somewhere around the 1880s. When their wives asked where they had been, they answered, "Nowhere." It stuck.

As cattle ranches sprang up around it, by the turn of the century Nowhere had grown into a bustling community with a general store, livery/blacksmith, two saloons, a church, a one-cell jailhouse, doctor's office, even a bank. The post office consisted of a few boxes tucked into a corner of Harland's General Store.

From spring to fall the mail came every week, but only twice over winter. That was mainly because of the road. Anyone traveling to Nowhere knew they were in for a bumpy ride. The rutted road received no maintenance unless some rancher got tired of his horse stumbling and went back with a shovel.

For years, Nowhere's population hovered around 150, give or take a baby being born or someone passing. Doc Fillmore's two-bed infirmary was in a back room of his home on Third Street. There was no such thing as an undertaker. Families built their loved ones' coffins and dug the graves themselves.

Folks from outlying ranches came into town for their provisions on Saturdays. During the day, the little stores would buzz with activity. Not so the saloons. Avoided by families with children, they sat idle until after sundown, when the ranch hands were finished with their work.

The constable in Nowhere was a middle-aged ex-soldier by the name of Bert Crumbly. Bert didn't have much to do. Ranch hands got drunk and fought with their fists, not guns. Knowing tempers would be fueled by firewater on a Saturday night, their foremen made sure the boys left their guns in the bunkhouse before heading into town. Every other week or so, one of them would land in Bert's jail or one of Doc's beds. The next morning, he'd wake up with a hangover or some stitches and be shooed out the door to wander the streets. Patched up, sobered up, or both, he would seek out the previous night's adversary and apologize.

In '27, a scrawny kid barely in whiskers rumbled into Nowhere in a beat-up Model A. He was there to rob the bank. To ensure a quick getaway, he left the motor running while he carried out his crime. It was a foolish move. An automobile was a rare sight in Nowhere, and the coughing, sputtering contraption soon drew a knot of curious onlookers.

Inside the bank, Berry Milburn was looking down the barrel of an old Colt he thought must have been left over from the Civil War. The boy robber's hand shook so badly the teller knew he was going to die, if only by accident. Then Berry saw there were no bullets in the cylinder. He handed the robber fifty dollars and told him that's all he had. From the looks of the kid, Berry figured if he came over the counter he could take him.

Stuffing the bills in his pocket, the kid backed out of the

lobby into the street. The three elderly men and two ladies gathered around the Model A scattered when they saw the pistol. Waving it at them, the robber jumped in the car. Panicked, he pumped the clutch and ground the gears. One of the old men pulled out his .44. and sent a bullet through the door, missing the robber's left knee by an inch. The kid screamed like a scared little girl and shoved the accelerator to the floor. He was gone, taking the only road out of town.

Alerted by the gunshot, Constable Crumbly jumped on his horse and took off, following the tire tracks at a gallop. "His gun's not loaded, Bert!" he heard Berry yell behind him. Bert found the kid three miles out, trying to fix a flat.

Darting in front of the automobile, the young robber poked his head above the hood and pointed his Colt at the lawman. With his arms folded over the saddle horn, Bert calmly asked, "What's your name, son?"

The kid looked surprised to be asked. "Billy Jackson," he answered in a petulant tone.

"Billy, put that gun down. We both know it ain't loaded. I'm not fixin' to shoot you less'n I got to." Straightening up in the saddle, Bert unholstered his own Colt and held it at his side. "Then I'll just wing you in the arm or the leg, whichever presents the better opportunity." He gestured toward the automobile with the barrel of the .44.

Tossing his pistol on the front seat, Billy raised his hands and stood there sniveling and gulping. Big tears ran down his cheeks. Burt climbed down from his horse and ambled toward him. "C'mon, I'll help you fix the dang tire." He ended up doing it himself while the would-be crook sat wailing at the roadside. Then Bert followed the boy back to town and escorted him into the bank. Mumbling an apology, Billy handed over the fifty to Milburn.

Instead of shackling the poor bugger, Burt took him home and put a plate of venison stew in front of him. The kid wolfed it down, pausing only long enough between bites to explain why he hadn't eaten in days. His father, Billy said, was laid up with a busted leg; they had no food and no money.

The kid could be lying but Bert didn't think so. He'd dealt with enough lawbreakers to know whether it was evil or hardship that drove them. After Billy finished his second plate of stew, Bert said, "We're going back to town."

By late afternoon just about everyone in town understood Billy's plight. Bert took him around and had him repeat it in every shop, saloon, even on the doorsteps of private homes. The pastor of the church promised to take up an offering for the family on Sunday and send some men out to help make repairs to the house.

Billy Jackson left Nowhere that evening in an automobile brimming with supplies. Thanks to Constable Bert and the people of Nowhere, the boy was lighthearted. He'd reached his turning point. Rather than pursue a life of crime, he would follow the straight and narrow and trust it to take him in the right direction. He went on to get educated and made a killing in oil. Years later he returned to Nowhere and repaid the townsfolk for their generosity. Everyone who remembered the kid who robbed the bank was amazed. Everyone, that is, but Bert.

Nowhere's economic decline began to pinch in April of 1938. The Great Depression was driving folks to slaughter their livestock for their own tables and coax vegetable gardens out of their dusty back yards. With the village streets all but deserted, merchants were closing shop early and going home to their hungry children. Travelers passing through became a thing of the past. The two sleeping rooms

Harland had built onto the back of his store sat vacant for months at a time.

One afternoon a stranger tooled into Nowhere in a shiny new gunmetal gray Buick Special. He braked in front of Harland's General Store, sending up a cloud of dust from under the car's fat whitewall tires. The few shoppers in Harland's store rushed out with their children for a look. Decked to the nines in a Stetson hat, fringed jacket and alligator boots, the portly man got out and stepped up on the running board. Gesturing to the small gathering to quiet down, he loudly announced, "Good people of Nowhere, I am Maurice Jenkins of Dallas, and I have come to make you rich."

A hush came over Jenkins' audience. The man who'd been kicking the Buick's tires stopped in mid-swing. A woman grabbed her son off the back bumper. Harland came out of his store and leaned against his porch rail to listen.

Distracted from his work on old Mrs. Mainer's roof, Bert climbed down the ladder to see what the commotion was about. He made his way over to Main Street just in time to hear Jenkins say, "Oil. That's right, my friends. O-I-L .That sticky, gooey stuff that makes anyone who touches it rich." His smile broadened like a Cheshire cat's. "You might even say *filthy* rich." Tossing back his head, he let out a hearty laugh.

"So yer a driller?" one of the elders asked, scrutinizing the nattily-dressed stranger with scrunched-up eyes. "You don't look like no driller."

Jenkins responded with a howl of derisive laughter that rattled the folks' teeth. "Not at all, my good man. I'm the guy who tells 'em where to build the rigs." Reaching into the automobile, he brought out some sort of apparatus, holding it high so everyone could see. "This, good people, is an oil spectrometer, a sophisticated device that detects the amount of oil in the ground. It has proven to be effective to a depth of five hundred eighty-nine feet."

His claim was met with titters. A boy in his late teens who was known around town to have above-average intelligence raised his hand to shush them. "It's true. I know all about that thing."

"How's it work then?" one of the men yelled.

"See this little spring here?" Maurice held out the device and pointed to its side. "When the spectrometer is placed on the ground, this spring activates a glass bead inside the cylinder. If there's oil under the ground, the bead rises to indicate how much. Let me demonstrate."

Maurice (known everywhere but Nowhere as Alfred Tanner, flim-flam man) placed the device on the ground beside the car. "Here's how it works." He held down a trigger hidden by a metal plate on the back. Motor oil poured into the cylinder, slowly raising the glass bead. At the same time, a small amount of oil was released from the bottom of the machine.

Maurice's mouth dropped. His eyes widened. "Yes, yes. Oh, my!" Grabbing the device, he jumped to his feet and scampered down the street. The boy who knew about spectrometers shouted, "Look!" The people turned their attention to the small puddle of oil on the ground next to the Buick.

An arthritic old-timer grimaced as he bent down and stuck his finger in it. "Yep," he confirmed as he grasped the fender to hoist himself up. "She be oil all right." Meanwhile, Maurice darted up and down the street like a jackrabbit, placing the spectrometer here and there and letting out a whoop to let them know it registered.

Word of the rich visitor with the miraculous oil meter spread fast. By the time Maurice stepped back onto the running board, the small group of spectators had become a big crowd. They waited while he caught his breath. Placing his hands on his hips, he announced the good news. "People of Nowhere, you are sitting on the one of the largest pools of oil in Texas."

Oil, my foot. More like snake oil. Bert had heard enough. Taking his badge from his pocket, he pinned it on his chest pocket, stepped forward and looked Jenkins in the eye. "May I see that device?"

"I'd like to accommodate you, sir." Jenkins' smile was as phony as his dulcet tone. "However, it's extremely delicate. Unless one knows how to handle it, its balance could be disturbed and it would take days to recalibrate." Reaching into the car, he pulled out a leather satchel and tucked the apparatus inside.

Stepping cautiously around Bert, Jenkins left the crowd to its musings and walked over to the porch where Carl Harland stood. Pointing to the sign in the store's front window, he asked, "Might you have a vacancy in your hotel, sir?"

"Ain't no hotel, Bud, just a couple of sleeping rooms in back," Carl said, punctuating his answer with a long stream of tobacco juice spat into the dirt.

"I see. Yes, that will do nicely. I take it you are Mr. Harland?" Maurice asked, extending his right hand.

"Carl, you can call me Carl," Harland answered with a friendly grin and a vigorous shake.

"Well, Carl, my friends call me Maury. And I can tell already you and I are going to be good friends."

Of all the people gathered in the street that afternoon, Bert was the one skeptic. As he stood listening to the townsfolk chattering excitedly about their prospects of fabulous wealth, the constable felt compelled to take action.

After dining with the Harlands, Jenkins sat picking his teeth in a wicker rocking chair on the store's front porch. Spotting him from across the street, Bert decided to pay him a visit."So, Maurice, traveled around Texas a lot, have you?"

"Oh yes, yes. Texas, Oklahoma, New Mexico. All over."

"Ever been to Huntsville?"

"Huntsville, Alabama? No, can't say as I have. Why do you ask?" Maurice avoided the lawman's gaze. Suddenly it seemed very warm on the porch. Sweat trickled down the yoke of his studded cowboy shirt.

Bert smirked."Oh, I think you know. Could it be because you look like a man who's spent time behind bars? And I think you know I'm talking about Huntsville Prison, not Alabama."

Bristling with indignance, Maurice stood from the chair. "I resent that." He raised his nose in the air, grasped the lapels of his jacket and stuck out his chest. "I'll have you know, sir, that I am a college graduate and an entrepreneur with an impeccable reputation."

Bert straightened up from leaning on the porch rail, walked over and pointed his finger in Jenkins' face. "Now you listen to me, Maurice or whatever your name is, and you listen good. I don't like you, I don't trust you. You steal one penny from one person in Nowhere and I will chase you to the ends of the earth. Do I make myself clear?"

"I assure you, sir, I have no intention of taking a thing from these dear people. My only objective is to help them survive this terrible economy." Jenkins, aka Tanner, sniffed. "Now if you'll excuse me, I'd like to turn in."

"I'm watching you, Jenkins. You just remember that," Bert warned as he descended the porch steps and headed toward the jailhouse.

Pacing his room, Alfred Tanner cursed a blue streak. His talent was conning people. The few he couldn't, he hated. All it took was one to unravel a scam. Yeah, he knew Huntsville, every nook and cranny of it. During the five years he was locked up there, he worked every lousy job from sorting stinking laundry to swabbing floors to slaving in that miserable hole of a kitchen. Sleep that night brought him nightmares of the place.

Tanner spent the next two days buzzing around the countryside plopping his spectrometer on the ground. A few ranchers ran him off, but he conned many into following him around like puppy dogs drooling over promises of mansions and limousines. There was a tense moment when one man thought he saw Tanner filling the device with oil. Nothing if not a smooth talker, Tanner easily convinced him he was just oiling the spring.

One of his encounters was with a rancher out on the far range. The man listened and watched, then asked about the expense of processing the oil once it was out of the ground. Jenkins' response was as slick as the stuff he was peddling. "My dear sir, that's hardly a concern. You see, when oil is drawn from the depths, the rocks and sand it passes through purify it." The rancher nodded. He was a cattleman, not a geologist.

Tanner kept busy with his con for three more days. On the third, he asked to use Harland's telephone. Telephones were scarce in Nowhere. With recovery from the Depression still a distant longing, most folks viewed it as a non-necessity. Having one of the few phones in town allowed Carl to charge his customers to use it. He divided his monthly cost among them and added what he felt was a fair service fee. Some months he came out ahead, but not by much and not often.

After Tanner hung up, Carl said nothing about a charge. It was worth paying it himself just to listen in to Tanner's end of the conversation. And Maurice spoke loudly enough for anyone in the store to hear. "Yes, yes, Arthur. Very possibly the biggest pool ever discovered. What? No. Just come right away. What? Drive all night, then. Just get here. No. Leave the crew in Dallas. And Arthur, not a word to anyone, understand? Oh, don't worry about that. If I have to, I'll finance it myself. See you in the morning."

Harland hurried to the rear of the store so Maurice wouldn't suspect he'd been listening. Tanner poked around until he found the store owner standing over a shipment of children's clothing he hadn't been able to sell. "Good news, Carl! I have a good friend who's a driller. He's coming down to evaluate our discovery."

Carl pursed his lips and sucked in his breath. This fellow Maury was going to make him rich. No more grubbing for a few dollars to get through the month. He could see himself in the finest suits, dressing his wife like a queen, eating in luxurious restaurants, traveling the world.
The bubble in Carl's head burst at the sound of Maurice's voice. "Would it be possible to have a meeting tonight with everyone involved?"

"Oh, sure, Maury. I'll put the word out. We can meet in the church. What time?"

"Let's say, seven-thirty? Thank you, Carl. You're going to be a very wealthy man. Richer even than Henry Ford." Maurice slapped Carl on the back and left. Whistling a cheery tune, Harland hung the "Back in 15 minutes" sign on the door and hurried off to spread the word.

The church was packed. Even the ranchers from the outlying areas made it in. Bert leaned against the back wall with his arms crossed, watching Tanner's every move.

Tanner aka Jenkins knew how to hold court. At times he sounded like a preacher, at others like a schoolteacher. Pointing to numerous spots surrounding Nowhere on a large map pinned to the wall, he held the crowd in thrall. "So you see, my friends, you are literally sitting on millions and millions of dollars." Now for the sucker punch. "I can guarantee you twenty-five percent of the profits."

A rancher leapt from his chair. "Wait a minute, Mister. We get twenty-five and you get seventy-five?"

"What are you trying to pull?" another shouted. People stood up and started yelling. Looking like a bewildered innocent, Maurice stood silent as the angry din grew louder. This was too perfect, exactly what he wanted.

"Ladies and gentlemen, please, please. Let me explain. I should have said that I would *like* to promise you twenty-five percent. However, sadly, I have been advised not to allow you to participate in this venture. Therefore, I will be financing the operation myself."

"Advised by who?" someone yelled. "Who told you that?"

"Why, your constable," Tanner said, looking squarely at Bert.

All eyes turned to glare at Bert. "Crumbly don't speak for me," one of the ranchers piped up, giving Bert a hard look. "He ain't got no say in the matter. He's the law, not my banker."

"Now hold on here," Bert said loudly enough for the entire assembly and Tanner to hear. He pushed himself away from the wall, squaring his shoulders and extending his six-foot frame to its full stature. "This guy breezes into town and you believe him because of a tiny spot of oil on the ground?"

"Whaddaya think, Crumbly, that it magically appeared under his boot?" a 50-ish, spectacled man quipped. "If that's the case, I'll dance a little jig and bring up a gusher." He started hopping from one foot to the other.

The hall erupted in laughter. Climbing the platform steps, Carl Harland rushed to the pulpit and hammered it with his fist. The place went quiet as everyone turned to look at him. This was the owner of the general store, one of the most highly regarded men in Nowhere.

"Friends, while we all know and respect Bert and he's always upheld the law, this has nothing to do with him. It's financial. This is our business. And here's one more thing. If you contribute to the cost of the drilling, you'll be entitled to a larger share of the profits. Do I have that right, Maurice?"

"Absolutely," Tanner said, relaxing now that his efforts were about to pay off. "While I am certainly able to pay the entire cost of the operation, I would prefer to share the wealth with you good people." A murmur of approval went up from the crowd.

Bert left the meeting in disgust. All these years he had looked out for them. Now they were letting greed blind them.

Folks began queuing up bright and early the next morning waiting for the bank to open. By 9:30, the vault was nearly empty. The president locked the door and sat mopping his brow in his office.

At 10 o'clock, Billy Bly, aka Arthur, pulled up in front of Harland's General Store in a gleaming new Chevrolet pickup. Tanner hopped in and they spent the next two days collecting signatures on worthless pieces of paper. The "contract" stated investors would receive 25 percent of the oil profits, 50 if they contributed to the cost of the drilling. Bert made the rounds, too, trying to warn off the citizens of Nowhere. His reward in most cases was a stern admonition to mind his own business and get off their property.

At two the following morning, Alfred Tanner and Billy Bly sneaked out of their rooms at the back of Harland's store. At eight, Carl went around to tell Maurice breakfast was just about over. Knocking and receiving no response, he called to him. Nothing. He pressed his ear against the door. Not a sound. Panicking, he ran to the spot at the back of the property where their vehicles should be. Empty. A worm of fear began to gnaw at Carl's brain and work its quiver through his body. The money he had entrusted to the oilmen included the reserve to purchase next month's supplies. If it was gone, so was his business.

Maybe they were out testing more land. That had to be it. No use stirring up the people. But since Arthur arrived, he and Maury hadn't missed a meal with Carl and the missus. Why was today different? Back in the store, Carl stood on wobbly legs staring out the window. Not one soul came in that morning. They had given all their money to the con men.

Doc came in around noon to take another look at the map. His eye caught Carl's shaking hands and glistening brow as he spread out the map on the counter. "What's the matter, Carl? Why do you have the shakes?"

Carl gave a little shrug and tried to make light of it. "Sure ain't from boozin', Doc." Doc wasn't laughing. He knew Carl to be a healthy man. Now the store owner put his hand over his eyes and hung his head. "I can't find them."

"What are you talking about? Can't find who?" Doc asked querulously.

"The oil men. They had supper with us last night. Arthur said his crew was on their way and they'd start drilling as soon as they got here. But there's no sign of them, Doc. I was up real early this morning and if the crew showed up I would've seen them. They're gone. I know it. They're gone, their cars are gone, our money is gone."

Doc came around the counter. "Oh, now, hold on my boy." He patted Carl's back. "Let's not go sounding the alarm bell just yet. I'm sure there's a reasonable explanation. Maybe they decided to go meet the men. You know they wanted to keep things quiet."

"I hope you're right, Doc. If not, I'm sunk." Carl sighed, then forced a shaky smile. "We'll wait a day and see what happens."

The day ended with no word from Maurice or Arthur. The next day passed and the next. One by one the people of Nowhere came to grips with the ugly truth that they'd been conned. It was a hard pill to swallow and all they could swallow. They barely ate, slept, worked or spoke. The wives found their voices soon enough, though. To escape their scolding, the men took to standing in the roadway praying to see a dust cloud moving toward them.

It didn't happen. Nothing happened until Bert came into Carl's store on day two and asked to use the phone. The morning of the third day, the dust cloud appeared. Hearing shouts, the people of Nowhere streamed out of their houses and shops and gathered in the street. Watching it draw closer, they laughingly chided each other for doubting the oilmen.

The crowd parted as the car approached. It soon became apparent that this was not the arrival of the oilmen. The boxy vehicle with the star on each side rolled to a stop in front of the bank. A tall, lanky, weathered man with a gold star on his khaki shirt emerged from the back seat. Bert stepped forward and shook the Ranger's hand. Murmurs traveled through the crowd. What was the officer's business in Nowhere?

"Them two was crooks, just like Bert said," one of the old men declared with a downcast expression. He had seen plenty in his 75 years, but this beat all.

The bank president opened the door and ushered the Ranger and Bert inside. The crowd milled anxiously and grew louder until the three of them emerged 20 minutes later. The Ranger held up his hand to quiet them.

"Folks, I'm Texas Ranger Mark Hailey with the Dallas regiment." He waited for the whispering to stop. "The so-called oilmen you knew as Maurice and Arthur are actually a couple of confidence men named Alfred Tanner and Billy Bly."

There were hoots of anger and disbelief. Some of the women began to weep. Bert shouted over them. "Now wait, folks! It's not all bad news."

Blood-red in the face, a stocky rancher yelled, "How could it not be? We've been hoodwinked out of every penny we had. We outta hunt them down and string 'em up!"

Hailey raised his voice. "No, sir. Your money is safe. It's in the bank." The crowd went silent. The only sound was the neighing of a horse over in the livery stable. "We've been watching these two for some time, knowing they'd pull another hoax. When they left here the other morning, we nabbed them right down the road."

"Bert tried to warn us they was crooks," Harland said with a sheepish glance at the constable.

"You folks are lucky to have Constable Crumbly watching out for you," Halley said. "He was a tremendous help to us. Not only did he alert us to his suspicions, he waited and watched all night and let us know as soon as Tanner and Bly took off." All eyes turned to Bert with gratitude and respect.

"What about them two fancy automobiles?"

"Stolen from a dealer in Fort Worth the day before Tanner showed up here," Hailey replied.

"So yer sayin' they didn't get our money after all?"

"Not a penny," Hailey said with a big grin.

"Hurray for Bert, outstanding Texas lawman!" someone shouted. The people cheered and applauded.

"I vote we put him on full time!" Harland said, leaving the crowd to stand next to Bert and drape his arm across Bert's shoulder.

Doc piped up, "I'll second that!"

The people of Nowhere returned to their homes, secure in the belief that the Lord and Constable Bert would continue to watch over them.

Ironically, several years later a massive pool of oil was discovered right where Tanner said it was. Even so, the people of Nowhere had long since learned their lesson about the pitfalls of greed. Their newfound wealth extended beyond their bank accounts to their hearts. From then on, Nowhere was known as the most giving town in Texas.

Earl

The shaft of sunlight bouncing off the shop's north wall distracted Earl Pennington. He straightened up, rubbed the small of his back and looked at the clock. Two-thirty already. Just one more bolt and he could pull the motor out of Grant Scudder's Model A and get it onto the bench. Then a couple of hours more to replace the rod and burnt piston. Earl heaved a sigh picturing the fit old Grant would pitch when he handed him the bill.

Grant had been Earl's first customer when Earl inherited the shop from his late father. The elder Mr. Pennington ran it as a blacksmith shop for years before automobiles came into existence. Old man Scudder was a stubborn cuss who burned up engines like they were kindling. Earl could never persuade him to check the oil regularly. "I put in three quarts two months ago," Grant would argue, shifting the ever-present broom straw from one side of his mouth to the other. "She don't need any for another month."

"Man, you just don't learn. You'll burn up the motor if you don't," Earl warned.

"Let 'er burn, then! I ain't doin' it!"

Grant was a speed demon. He loved nothing more than to

jam the accelerator to the floor and hold it there. His four horses were no match for the velocity and endurance of his automobiles. The animals were put out to pasture the day he bought the first Model A, and there they stayed. But Grant gave no quarter to the mundane tasks required to keep the vehicles running. That's was Earl's worry.

And so it went. This was the third engine Earl had worked on for the obstinate old goat. No skin off Earl's nose. For15 years now, Earl had repaired motors, transmissions, back ends and flat tires. He'd seen it all. Ol' Scudder didn't know it yet, but this one would set him back a few bucks. From the smell, Earl had a strong hunch that the motor was burnt. If it was beyond repair, he could drop in a junked one he had in the back of the shop. Sure, Grant would holler and threaten to push the car into the gully behind Earl's garage. He'd yell at Earl to just junk the thing, and stomp out like he had twice before. The next morning he would show up at the shop and ask if it was fixed.

"Nope. Maybe by this afternoon."

"Get 'er done then." Grant was too old for niceties.

Sensing movement, Earl wiped the grease off his hands and squinted through the grimy shop window. A Model A pickup sat in front of the Grabie house. Earl felt a surge of discomfort as a 30-ish couple he'd never seen before got out and looked around.

David Grabie died three weeks ago. Earl attended his funeral. It was one of the few times in his life anyone saw him in a suit. Earl missed his friend. Just about every afternoon, Dave would hobble over to Earl's shop. Seated in the kitchen chair just inside the door, the elderly gentleman would dispense advice, telling Earl how to repair whatever he was working on at the time. Earl only half listened. Dave was a genial soul, but he knew nothing about automobiles.

One day Dave failed to show at his regular time. Busy fixing a transmission, Earl didn't notice for a while. When he realized he was alone, he wiped his hands on an oily shop rag, crossed the road and climbed Dave's porch steps. "Dave! Ho, Dave, you all right?" Receiving no answer, Earl opened the screen door and stepped in. The old man was stretched out on the living room floor. Kneeling beside him, Earl felt for a pulse, even though he knew he wouldn't find one. The coolness of Dave's skin told Earl he'd been dead for hours.

Using Dave's phone, Earl called Central. It took several rings for Lucinda to come on the line. Earl could picture the middle-aged grandmother in curlers and filing her nails at the switchboard.

"Ticker gave out," Doc announced. "Been bad for a while."

So Earl went to the funeral, said goodbye to his only friend and went back to his shop. He left the kitchen chair where it was. Now and then he would forget Dave was dead and speak to him. Sometimes he did it deliberately, almost expecting an answer. For the most part, David Grabie was a quiet, shy man. Until he sat in that chair.

Earl watched as the man in Grabie's yard turned and looked

at the garage. Must be Dave's nephew, Earl thought. The woman said something. Earl couldn't make out her words but felt sure she was talking about him. Feeling guilty for spying, he returned to his work on Grant's engine.

He finished positioning the motor in the compartment, then rolled under the car on the creeper to bolt it to the transmission. Hearing a soft scuffing sound, he looked to his left and nearly bumped his nose on the tip of a tiny Buster Brown oxford. The shoes were attached to a pair of short legs enclosed in sharply-creased khakis. Puzzled but determined to finish the job, Earl tightened the last two bolts. A brown-haired, blue-eyed, small boy's head suddenly appeared sideways under the running board. He grinned at Earl, showing a gap where two teeth had been. His round face reminded Earl of a cherub's.

"What are you doing?" the boy lisped. Earl thought he couldn't be more than six or seven.

Grasping the running board's edge, Earl rolled himself out from under. He stood up and wiped his hands on a rag. Not that it did much good. His nails were caked with grease, his hands permanently stained. Looking up at Earl with a cocked head and precocious grin, the boy stuck out his hand. "How do you do, sir? I am Thomas Nelson the third. And what would your name be?" The words whistled through the gap in his teeth.

Earl rubbed vigorously at his index finger and thumb before bending over to grasp the tiny hand. "Name's Earl. I work on automobiles."

"Pleased to meet you, Mr. Earl," the boy replied. "We just moved into the house across the street."

Earl felt oddly as he had that time he was hauled before the judge. "Across the road," he corrected.

"Pardon?"

"Out here in the country we call 'em roads. Streets are in the city," Earl explained, and for all he cared they could keep them there.

"Of course. How silly of me," Thomas said. "What exactly malfunctioned on this automobile, Mr. Earl?"

Malfunctioned? "Engine burnt," Earl told the pint-sized vocabularian simply.

"There you are!" The pair turned to the voice's owner. A slim, attractive woman with shiny brown hair and sparkling green eyes stood in the doorway. For a moment Earl thought his ex-wife had returned. He shook his head to clear the vision. The woman's smile seemed to light up her entire face. "Thomas, are you going to introduce me to your friend?"

"Yes, Mother. Sorry. This is Mr. Earl. He works on automobiles. Mr. Earl, this is my mother," the boy said.

The woman held out a delicate hand, stunning Earl speechless at the sight of the glittering gemstone rings gracing three of her fingers. "Pleased to meet you, Mr. Earl," she said, flashing a brilliant white smile. "We just moved in, or I should say are moving in, to my husband's uncle's house across the street. My husband and I both grew up in the country. We felt this would be the best environment for Thomas."

"Road, Mother," Thomas said. "Out here they are known as roads."

"Of course. I knew that. Come along, Thomas. It's almost time for dinner."

"Perhaps Mr. Earl would like to join us," Thomas suggested, as if it were the most common thing in the world to invite a mechanic to supper.

Earl glanced down at his greasy uniform and shoved his grimy, oil-caked hands into his pockets. "I…can't. I gotta finish this here automobile." His ears burned with the lie. The engine was good as new until Grant seized it up again.

"Perhaps another time. After we've settled in. How about this Saturday evening?" Thomas's mother, whose name was Alice, said.

"I… I'll let you know," Earl stammered, feeling as awkward as a schoolboy. He was mortified that he hadn't shaved for days and sure that his breath stunk. He backed up until he bumped into the Model A. The gentle breeze blowing through the garage wafted the woman's perfume his way. "I'll see what I can do." That was as much of a commitment as he dared make.

"Well, I hope you can join us. We'll look forward to it, won't we, Thomas?"

"Oh, indeed we will. However, I'm sure we will see each other before then. Goodbye, Mr. Earl."

"Goodbye," Earl murmured. He stepped to the door of the garage and watched them stroll hand-in-hand toward Dave's house.

Earl hadn't been invited to anyone's home since Mattie left him five years ago. She always said she couldn't stand Earl touching her with his greasy hands. So every night he'd spend no less than 20 minutes washing his face and scrubbing his hands and nails until there was not a speck of grease to be found. He'd even change his clothes before going back to the house. It made no difference. She left him anyway.

Earl looked around the shop and was dumbfounded that these aristocratic city slickers would invite him to dinner. The place was shameful. Tools were scattered all over the floor and bench. A grease-caked wrench and a ratchet lay in the doorway where customers had to step over them. An old engine lay rusting in the corner. Filthy rags were strewn everywhere.

Earl's house wasn't any better. Dirty dishes and empty cans littered every surface in the kitchen. Unwashed clothes lay in a smelly heap in the bedroom. When was the last time he took a bath? Last week or the week before? He couldn't remember. His face burned. To that boy and his mother he must have looked like a bum. Yet they treated him with respect.

"She done?" Earl jumped like he'd been shot. Grant

Scudder stood in the doorway.

"Yup," Earl said, recovering quickly. "That'll be thirty dollars."

"Thirty!" Grant shouted. "It was ten last time."

"Last time I didn't have to pull the engine and replace a piston," Earl answered peevishly, stifling the urge to tell the old man what he really thought.

"Next time I'll take it to Bixby," Grant sputtered.

"I'll haul 'er there for you for three bucks. And if you do what you're s'posed to there won't be a next time," Earl countered. He hoped Grant would take it to Bixby and find out what this work was really worth. Nevertheless, he added, "Don't go off half-cocked, Grant. The guy in Bixby will charge you half again as much. Then what? Tow it to Indianapolis where they'll soak you for double?"

Grant quieted down and looked at Earl as if seeing him for the first time. Grousing to himself, he handed Earl three bills. Once in the driver's seat, he hollered, "Crank 'er over for me!" The Model A started on the second go-around. Grant backed it out and took off down the road, driving at a reasonable speed until he was out of Earl's sight.

Closing shop for the day, Earl spent the next hour picking up and throwing away clutter and junk that had been piling up for years. That done, he washed the inside of the window. He'd wash the outside tomorrow morning before the sun came around.

145

Exhausted, Earl locked up and walked to the house. No rest for the weary. His home sweet home had all the ambiance of the town dump and stunk like rotten meat. He went from room to room opening every window. Carrying in buckets of water, he filled a kettle on the cook stove and straightened up the place while it heated. Dumping half of it into the sink, he washed, dried and put away the dishes, pots and pans. Next he scrubbed the floor, all the time hoping Master Thomas Nelson III wouldn't pick this time to visit.

At seven, Earl went looking for the galvanized tub. It was right where he left it, behind the house full of spare auto parts. Dragging it over to the shop, he arranged the parts neatly on the shelves. Back at the house, he placed the tub in the middle of the kitchen and heated more water. After his first bath, he stood staring incredulously at the white scum sloshing on top of black water. He heated more water and hopped back in with his razor. It chewed at his face. "That's what you get for not shaving for a week," he told the man in the mirror. Bathing finally done, he stuffed his filthy clothes into a laundry bag and stashed it behind the couch. He would wash them tomorrow. Finally, he stripped the bed of its grimy sheets and put on clean.

The next morning Earl arose early and washed everything he could get wet. At the clothesline, he watched Edward Nelson exit Dave's house wearing an impeccably tailored pinstripe suit and carrying a briefcase. The handsome man turned and kissed the equally attractive Alice. Their son stood in the doorway rubbing sleep out of his eyes. Waving to them, Edward started up the pickup and drove away.

The day dragged. With no automobile repairs on tap, Earl scrubbed the work bench while soaking his tools in gasoline. Once finished, he brought in his own automobile and puttered with the bent hinge on the back door. Earl rarely drove the car. Nowhere to go.

Throughout the day, Earl caught glimpses of Thomas, first sweeping the front porch with a broom much taller than him and later making a fort out of some old washtubs Dave kept behind the house. Around two, Earl remembered his laundry and, finding everything dry, began taking it down.

"They smell like sunshine and fresh air, don't they, Mr. Earl?"

Who else but Thomas could make ragged curtains and stained towels seem so important? Earl looked down at the little boy with the angelic smile. What was it about this child that stirred his cold heart? He smiled back. "That they do. They smell like the first day of spring after a long winter."

"I came to get you because there's a gentleman waiting in your shop," Thomas said. "I believe he wants you to inspect his automobile. You may not wish to, though."

Amused, Earl asked why. "He is Mr. John Dillinger," Thomas informed simply.

"Is that right?" Bright as he was, the boy had to be mistaken. By all accounts, Dillinger was 200 miles away. "Let's go see," Earl said.

Earl entered the garage with a spring in his step and

stopped short. His heart thumped and his breath caught in his throat.

"She started knocking coming out of Bixby. Mind taking a look at it?" the man asked with a smarmy grin.

"Uh, Shh…sure." Earl felt sweat beading his brow. "Thomas, run along home now."

"Mr. Earl is the best mechanic around," Thomas declared, a little too assertively for Earl's comfort.

The man glanced at Thomas with a patronizing grin. "Well, if that's so, why don't you stick around for the show? Just sit over there and watch." The man looked expectantly at Earl, who gazed back at him in silence. It was him, all right. Earl had seen that face many times in the newspaper and on the post office wall. None other than John Dillinger was asking–no, demanding–Earl to fix his getaway car.

Thomas hoisted himself onto the kitchen chair, swinging his legs back and forth. "Mr. Dillinger, are you going to shoot us if Mr. Earl can't fix your car?"

Unamused, Dillinger leaned on the fender and stared coldly at Earl. He pushed back his coat, exposing the pistol in his belt. "Why son, you've got me mixed up with somebody else. My name is Brown," Dillinger answered, never taking his eyes off Earl.

Thomas smiled coyly at Public Enemy Number One. "Nope. I've seen your picture in the newspaper numerous times. Why do you rob banks, sir?" Despite marveling at the kid's moxie, Earl shuddered.

"Because that's where they keep the money." Dillinger's darkly handsome face hardened as his patience wore thin. "I need the automobile now," he snapped at the mechanic.

"I...it's probably the spark plug wire. I got a new one right here."

"Don't try anything."Dillinger fingered the pistol in his waistband.

"But Mr. Dillinger, it's not *your* money," Thomas counseled.

"Look kid, just sit there and keep still," Dillinger shot back.

Fifteen tense minutes passed. "Try it now," Earl said, praying he'd been right about the wire. Keeping an eye on the mechanic, Dillinger got behind the wheel. The motor caught on the first try and hummed smoothly, not a hiccup.

"Much obliged, fella." Slamming shut the door, Dillinger backed the car out of the garage, tossing a bill at Earl as he did. It floated down and landed beneath the tool bench.

Wordlessly, man and boy watched the bank robber disappear over the hill. Earl took out his bandana and wiped his brow with shaking hands. His voice trembled. "Sure glad that's over. Hope he don't come back."

"I as well. I understand he's very dangerous," Thomas commented as casually as if he were talking about the weather. If he was frightened by the ordeal, he didn't show it.

They went looking for the bill. Spotting it first, Thomas snatched it off the floor and held it up to Earl. One hundred dollars. "You have to give it back, Mr. Earl," the boy said. "I'll reimburse you from my allowance."

Reimburse? Earl stifled a chuckle. "No, no. No need for that. You're right, though, Thomas. I will give it back."

"I should go home now," Thomas said. "Please remember you're joining us for dinner tomorrow evening. I believe Mother said six. Is that convenient? Oh, and Mr. Earl, Mother and Father will be upset when I tell them about Mr. Dillinger. Will you please assure them that I was perfectly safe?"

Earl couldn't help but grin. "Yes, Thomas, I will be there and I'll tell them."

All the next day, Earl debated whether to wear his suit or just a clean shirt and pants. He was vexed, having neither the nerve to go or beg off. That morning he did an oil change, fixed a flat and plugged a radiator. He closed the shop at noon and went home to take another bath and trim his hair with a pair of dull scissors.

At 5:30, he sat in his kitchen watching the clock. He looked at his hands again. He had scrubbed them with a brush doused in gasoline and scraped under his nails with an ice pick. They were as clean as they were going to get. He still felt grubby. He was a mechanic, after all. Thomas's father, he had learned, was an attorney. Earl stood and smoothed his jacket and trousers. A hand-me-down from his father, the suit was slightly threadbare and shiny in the knees and seat. Hoping they wouldn't notice, Earl straightened the tie he'd retrieved from the corner where he tossed it after Dave's funeral.

At 5:55, Earl crossed the road and climbed the Nelsons' porch steps. He raised his hand to knock, nearly planting his knuckles on Edward's nose as his host threw open the door. Seeming not to notice, Edward flashed a toothy smile and gave Earl a little bow. "Welcome, Mr. Pennington." He stuck out his hand.

Earl hesitated to take Edward's soft, lily-white hand in his calloused one. But he didn't want to appear unfriendly. He clasped the man's hand and gave it a quick shake. "Earl, just call me Earl."

"Come in, Earl. I believe dinner is just about ready." Kneading his clammy palms with his fingertips, Earl followed Edward through the living room. When they reached the archway to the dining room, Edward stopped, leaned in and whispered in Earl's ear. "Thomas and I have decided to not speak of the incident with Mr. Dillinger to my wife. It would be upsetting to her. However, I did alert the police and was told that about three hours after leaving here he was sighted fifty miles away. Earl, you kept my son safe. Thank you." Earl nodded and said nothing.

The table was set with fine china and highly-polished silverware. A vase of fresh flowers graced the middle of the linen covered table. Pulling out a chair, Thomas said, "Please sit here, Mr. Earl."

"I'll join you in just a minute," Alice called from the kitchen. Earl feasted his eyes on the heaping platter of roast beef, bowls of steaming vegetables and napkin-lined baskets of flaky dinner rolls at each end of the table. He felt like a king being served a banquet in his honor.

After they all were seated, Edward and Alice reached for Earl's and Thomas's hands on opposite sides of the table. It felt strange to Earl to hold a woman's hand if only to thank God for their food. After the prayer, Alice circled the table, filling each plate. His embarrassment overridden by his appetite, Earl watched her pile his with twice as much as the others.

Joining in haltingly at first, Earl soon found himself becoming comfortable with the conversation. He felt relaxed as he explained the intricacies of repairing a motor at length while his hosts listened with rapt attention. To Earl's surprise and delight, the evening turned out to be thoroughly enjoyable.

The following afternoon, Earl found himself smiling and humming even as he struggled to align the steering on a Ford. Sunday mornings were usually spent doing odd jobs or work left over from Saturday. This morning was different. Earl had accompanied Thomas and his parents to their church. It was the first time in 20 years he attended a service. It wasn't that he was hostile to religion, just neglectful. But this morning he enjoyed the choir and found the pastor's sermon insightful and uplifting.

Edward became a frequent visitor to the shop. There was a lot Earl wanted to know about the Bible, and he would pepper Edward with questions while busying his hands with a transmission or some other job. If Edward didn't know an answer, he would find it out and tell Earl the next time. One day when Earl asked how he could know the Lord, Edward happily led him to Christ. Thomas was overjoyed to hear that Earl had invited Christ into his heart. The following Sunday, Earl joined the church.

Over the next few weeks, Earl's and Thomas's friendship deepened. Fascinated with Earl and the work he did, the boy would visit the shop nearly every afternoon. Thomas liked to talk, but when it was clear that Earl was concentrating, he would sit quietly in the kitchen chair and just watch. He never offered advice as Dave had. Mr. Earl knew what he was doing.

One day as Thomas was leaving, he said, "Mr. Earl, I have learned so much from observing you, I believe I could take an automobile apart and put it back together again myself."

Earl stopped working and turned to the boy. "Thomas, it don't take no smarts to work on automobiles. Listen to me and listen good. You're sharp-witted. You take what God gave you and you go out and change the world. You hear what I'm sayin'?"

"I do. Oh, there's Father. He's home early," Thomas said. Hopping down from the kitchen chair, he dashed out and ran to greet Edward.

Grant Scudder was late. He had just 25 minutes to get to the mill, buy the feed and be home in time for supper. He stomped the gas pedal to the floor. The Model T shuttered. The speedometer climbed to 40, then 43."Come on!" Grant yelled. He swung around the curve, tipping the car. It scared Grant, but he chuckled a little as it righted itself. He kept his foot on the accelerator, practically standing on it. Straining, the engine whined.

Approaching Earl's shop at top speed, Grant caught a flash of movement. Normally careful to watch for automobiles, Thomas was running in the middle of the road back to Earl's shop. He hadn't said goodbye. Grant stomped on the brakes. Hearing squealing tires bearing down on him, Thomas froze. The Model A fishtailed in the loose gravel, sliding sideways.

Bolting from the shop at the din of calamity, Earl dived at the boy with his arms outstretched. He hit Thomas in the side, knocking the wind out of him. The boy went airborne and fell at the edge of the road, tumbling three times and landing in the ditch.

The last emotion Earl felt on this earth was relief to see the boy scramble to his feet unhurt. A millisecond later, Grant's runaway automobile skidded into Earl, catapulting him 50 feet down the road. Screaming and blubbering, Thomas ran to his friend. "Oh, Mr. Earl, I'm sorry. I'm so sorry." Broken and bloodied, Earl reached up to stroke the tears flowing down the little boy's cheeks. Then Earl's eyes fluttered shut and he died.

"I couldn't stop," Grant whimpered as he stumbled up and gasped at the sight of Earl's body.

"It was my fault," Thomas sobbed, choking out the words as he caressed Earl's arm. "My fault."

Rushing to the scene, Edward scooped up his son. "Are you hurt?" he asked anxiously as he checked the boy over.

Thomas twisted around in his father's arms and pointed at Earl. "Do something for Mr. Earl, Daddy! Do something!" he cried hysterically.

Edward hugged his son to his chest. Murmuring softly, he tried to comfort the child. "Mr. Earl is with the Lord now, Thomas." Turning to take Thomas's eyes away, Edward carried the boy to the porch and placed him in the arms of his weeping mother. "Alice, take him inside and call the police."

Earl looked down at his crumpled body lying in the road. "Time to go, Earl," he heard David Grabie say. Earl looked at his friend in amazement. Dave's countenance was that of a man in his 30s, not the withered old soul Earl last saw lying in a casket. Together they walked into eternity.

The entire congregation attended Earl's funeral. Grant Scudder stood in the back of the church with his head bowed throughout the entire service. After the police cleared him of any wrongdoing, he fulfilled the promise he made to Earl each time Earl repaired his automobile. Attaching his buckboard's harness to the Model A's front bumper, he urged his horses forward until the automobile toppled into the gully behind Earl's garage.

∾

The man in the impeccably tailored pin-stripe suit stood staring at the headstone. Taking the white handkerchief from his breast pocket, he dabbed at his cheeks. Approaching him tentatively, the cemetery caretaker asked with a kindly smile, "Can I help you, young man?"

Thomas turned to look at the elderly man. "No thank you, sir. I was just reminiscing about an old friend."

"Then I'll leave alone you, son. If you need anything, just let me know."

Thomas nodded. The caretaker tottered over to tidy up the third row of gravesites. Thomas knelt at the headstone. The inscription read:

EARL PENNINGTON
1886-1934

HE GAVE HIS LIFE THAT

OTHERS MIGHT LIVE

"Thank you." Thomas said simply. That afternoon in the Mercy Hospital emergency room, Dr. Thomas Nelson III saved the life of a child, the victim of a traffic accident.

Dear Reader:

Thank you for investing your time in reading *Tales from My Back Porch.* I hope it was an enjoyable experience. Did you find the secret hidden in the tales? The secret, which is not really hidden, is that each one of us is living a story. From birth to death, our lives touch so many. We can't help but influence those around us. It is my wish that you read this book from time to time and realize that your life is of great value.

May our God richly bless you.

ABOUT THE AUTHOR

Darrell Case is the author of nine books. The tenth is in the works and will be released in the spring of 2018. He and his wife, Connie, live in central Indiana. For more information about Darrell's writings free books and other offers visit: www.darrellcase.com

www.ingramcontent.com/pod-product-compliance
Lightning Source LLC
Chambersburg PA
CBHW060426130626
46555CB00005B/2240